9

THE GIRLS OF CANBY HALL

BOY TROUBLE

EMILY CHASE

SCHOLASTIC INC.
New York Toronto London Auckland Sydney

ISBN 0-590-40377-X

12 11 10 9 8 7 6 5 4 3 2 1   6 7 8 9/8 0/9

Printed in the U.S.A.   06

THE GIRLS
OF CANBY HALL

BOY
TROUBLE

THE GIRLS
OF CANBY HALL

CHAPTER ONE

I will be generous," Shelley Hyde declared. She turned away from the makeup mirror on her bureau at which she was experimenting with a new eye shadow and held it out to her roommate, Dana Morrison. "*You're* the glamorous one," she said. "*You* take the green-gold iridescent."

Dana — thin, sleek, a New York girl — was standing in the middle of the room — their room, Room 407, Baker House, Canby Hall — and looking at the books and notebooks piled on her desk. She was holding her Number Four favorite superlong sweater, which happened to be the exact color of her green eyes, but she was not moving, not putting it on, even though she had a date with Randy Crowell almost immediately. Dana shook her head at Shelley's offer. "I don't feel very glamorous," she said. "I feel as though if I don't get this book report started . . . and

1

I haven't even looked at my Spanish assignment. . . ."

"Hey, don't talk about schoolwork, Dana. It's Friday," Shelley said as she turned back to the mirror. In the bright light of the circle of bulbs, she studied her round face with its bright blue eyes, their lids heavy with the green-gold glitter she had wanted to give to Dana. After a while, she fluttered her eyes, sucked in her cheeks, pursed her lips, and pulled her short, thick, blonde curls back from her forehead. Finally, she sighed.

"Nothing works," she said. "I'm always going to look like Country Girl, Iowa, USA."

"You *are* from Iowa," Dana said with a distracted air, her mind clearly someplace else. "You know what, Shel?" she said, more firmly. "I don't feel like keeping my date with Randy tonight. I can't have a good time if that book report keeps whispering, 'Do me, do me, do me'."

"Not to worry," Shelley answered. "A louder voice will shout, 'Tomorrow, tomorrow, tomorrow'!" Shelley laughed at her own joke, then flung a hand in the air and launched into a dramatic recitation. "In the words of William Shakespeare, 'Tomorrow and tomorrow and tomorrow creeps in this petty pace from day to day till the last syllable of. . . .' "

Dana groaned. "Have you ever thought about becoming an actress?" she asked.

They both laughed. Shelley wanted almost

nothing else in the whole world. The acting bug had bitten her when she tried out for the spring play the year before. The infection had grown even more virulent over the past summer after she took a "Scenes from Shakespeare" workshop during Canby Hall's optional one-month summer term.

Dana ambled past her desk to the window. Outside, evening was happening quickly — a crisp, early winter darkness dimmed the trees in the park across from the dorm and shadows fell on the long driveway leading from the entrance gates of Canby Hall around the park, past the three school dormitories. Randy was probably driving his old pickup truck through the gates this very minute, she thought. Yes, she could see the gray shape of a truck taking the curve, coming closer, almost arriving at Baker House.

"There he is!" she exclaimed. "Always on time. Uff, I'm not even a bit ready." Dana's voice was muffled as she drew the sweater over her head. She shook her long, brown hair free, then combed it with her fingers so it fell straight and silky over her cheek. "I honestly wish I didn't have this date."

Shelley turned away from the mirror and faced her roommate.

"Dana, *what* are you talking about? You've got a whole weekend to work if you want to. When's that book report due anyway?"

"I can't help the way I feel," Dana murmured.

A tap at the door and a girl's voice. "Dana Morrison, visitor downstairs."

Shelley thrust Dana's down jacket into her hands and pushed her out the door. "Here's your coat, what's your hurry?"

"And forget about books," Shelley shouted down the hallway to her roommate's back.

With Dana on her way and Room 407 all hers, Shelley decided to do her elephant exercise. She bent over as much as her slight chubbiness permitted and, keeping her legs straight and her arms loose, walked swaying, lumbering, around the room. It was excellent exercise for the hips, she believed. "Hi," she said to the framed photograph of her parents as she passed the bureau.

It was nice, once in a while, to have absolutely nothing special to do, Shelley thought as she elephant-walked a few steps further. She was going to have a great evening. She'd try some more eye shadow colors, wash her hair, maybe start one of the romance novels she had borrowed from Cheryl Stern down the hall.

She straightened up, wrapped herself more snugly in her pink bathrobe, and went over to the bureau again. "Hello to you, too, my darling Paul," she said to the third framed picture, and "Hi, Tom," she whispered to the unframed snapshot that leaned against the picture of Paul. She gazed for a moment at the pictures of both boys, thinking about life and love and her roommates.

Dana had Randy, whom she liked very much

and Faith Thompson, their third roommate, a self-contained, terrific black girl from Washington, D.C. who was going to be a professional news photographer, was becoming really serious about her boyfriend, Johnny Bates. Only Shelley was twice in love. She had two boyfriends. She loved Paul Clifford from back home in Pine Bluffs and she loved Tom Stevenson, the most talented actor Greenleaf High ever had, and the most attractive boy she almost ever had seen including, and yet not including, Paul.

Sometimes Shelley got emotionally tangled being in love both long-distance and nearby. That evening, though, she felt emotionally just fine. She had got a letter from Paul in the morning's mail and tomorrow, Saturday night, she'd be seeing Tom. Tonight was nice and free for hair-washing, hanging around. Maybe she wouldn't stay alone reading Cheryl's novel after all. Maybe, later on, she'd stroll down the hall and join up with anybody else who was hanging around.

Shelley went to the footlocker in the middle of the room. It was the girls' storage cupboard and snack table. She opened the footlocker, took out a package of chocolate crackers, a jar of peanut butter, and a box of marshmallows, and happily began to make her favorite sandwich, the one she really could make only when she was alone. Dana and Faith puffed their cheeks out, put their fingers to their mouths, and made awful noises when she created and ate in their presence her marshmallow-and-peanut-butter sandwich on chocolate crackers. Shelley knew her roommates just wanted to help her to keep the pounds off, but one of the few advantages of having almost had a real problem about not eating last year was that she could now eat chocolate crackers from the Greenleaf supermarket as well as her mother's cookies from home once in a while without feeling guilty.

Dana dropped her down coat at the top of the stairs. She wasn't going out, she decided. The book report came first. Walking down the stairs and into the lounge to tell Randy, she was sure he wouldn't mind. He would know, just as she did, that her having to break their date had nothing to do with him. She felt good about her feelings for Randy, about their feelings for each other — not quite love, but deep friendship growing steadily more deep and solid. Randy was easy, amiable, *there*. He'd understand completely.

He was seated in one of the big chairs in the lounge. To her surprise, she found herself feeling nervous, edgy, even a little shaky as he unwound from the chair and began to come toward her with his long, loping stride. He covered the space between them in about four steps. For the hundredth time, Dana noticed how his pale gold hair curled, too long, over the collar of his denim workshirt, and how

that shining hair, his thin nose, the high cheek-
bones and line of his jaw all went together so
perfectly. Randy was one of the most beautiful
boys she'd ever seen, not just handsome but
beautiful. In that moment they walked toward each other, she smiled warmly but sadly.

He put his hands out and took her two
hands. "What's wrong?" he said immediately.
"What's the matter?"

It wasn't right that he was so perceptive,
Dana thought, strangely annoyed. Randy
Crowell was an outdoors, country boy. When
he graduated high school, he had decided he
was more interested in spraying his family's
apple orchards than in going to college. He
was from the old landowning Crowell family,
and he preferred checking up on the colts in
his father's horse breeding operations to
checking out a good ballet or funky flea
markets, Dana's big-city passions. It was almost
discomforting that Randy seemed to tune in
on her feelings faster and more accurately
than the city-smart boys she knew.

"Randy, this is going to sound awful but
there's nothing I can do about it. I can't go to
the movies with you tonight. I have a book
report that I absolutely have to do." Dana's
throat felt dry.

He looked down at her with steely gray eyes.
"But honey . . ." he began.

"I know. It's so terribly late," she said
quickly. "I wanted to telephone you as soon

as I realized . . . but, well, you know the way this dorm phone is always busy . . . then it was too late. . . ." Dana paused.

"I'm darn disappointed. I want to be with you. I don't want to go to a movie by myself," he said.

Dana, surprised at the tone in his voice, looked at him sharply. Suddenly, unexpectedly, she saw in the beautiful seventeen-year-old the little boy Randy must have been when he was five or six. She saw a golden-haired little boy confused and hurt, standing with arms hanging heavy at his sides, gray eyes wide, puzzled. He looked vulnerable, as though he had been told he had done something wrong and didn't know what it was. The little boy disappeared quickly when Dana hugged her tall boyfriend and smiled at him. She felt ashamed of herself.

"Randy, listen. I honestly can't go to the movie with you, but I just thought of something. Don't move one step. Promise?"

He shrugged and nodded and Dana raced out of the lounge, up the stairs, through the hallway, into Room 407. Shelley, startled, looked up from her marshmallow sandwich.

"Oh, Shel, you've got to help me," Dana exclaimed.

"Sure. How?" Shelley answered instantly.

"Go to the movies with Randy."

"What?"

"You go to the movies with Randy instead of me," Dana said.

"Absolutely not, Dana."

"Look, I really cannot go out tonight, not when I have that book report. But you can," Dana said.

"No way," Shelley insisted. "I'm washing my hair."

"Please, Shel. I hate to make him go alone."

"Dana, sometimes I think you're not as smart as you think you are. Will you please turn around and go downstairs and go out with your boyfriend?"

"I can't. I really can't," Dana said. "You have to go."

Shelley put her sandwich down but shook her head.

"Look," said Dana, "aren't we roommates?"

"Yes."

"Doesn't that mean we're like sisters?"

Shelley agreed. "But Dana," she added, "I honestly don't want to go out tonight."

"Shel, *please*."

Shelley had an unexpected thought. "Would you want me to if it were Michael?" she asked. Earlier that winter, Dana had had a tremendous crush on Dr. Michael Frank, the Canby Hall psychologist; it had been hard on everybody — her room-mates and her boyfriend particularly.

"Shel, that's not fair," Dana protested. "It's not the same thing at all. Yes, I acted like a nerd about Michael and yes, I was awful to Randy while it was going on but that doesn't have anything to do with this."

Shelley didn't answer.

Dana hunkered down next to the footlocker. "Listen, Shel, I have to do that report
but I don't want to lose Randy, not after it
took me so long to come back to my senses
about him. If he goes away alone now, I don't
think he'll want to see me again."

"Dana, this is a dumb discussion," Shelley
said.

"I beg you to go with him," Dana said.

Shelley finally accepted the fact that her
roommate was serious. She looked at the
marshmallow and chocolate cracker sandwich
in her hand and sighed. Then she looked at
Dana.

"Well," she said hesitantly. "Let's put it this
way. What movie?"

"*The Grapes of Wrath.* It's playing at the
revival theater."

"That's the old classic about Okies and the
Depression. Did you really want to see it?"
Shelley asked, surprised.

Dana giggled, smiled. "Not particularly,"
she said.

"I do happen to want to, and Tom doesn't,"
Shelley said.

"Well, then, perfect. See it with Randy."

Shelley sighed. "Okay," she said.

"Great, and thank you. Shelley dear, please
feel perfectly free to borrow my Anne Klein
scarf any time you want to." With that, Dana
turned brisk. "Now, put down that terrible

sandwich, put yourself together for the great outdoors and let's go and tell Randy."

"He'll be thrilled," Shelley said sarcastically, but Dana didn't notice.

The two girls came together into the lounge where Randy was sitting, waiting. He wasn't doing anything else except sitting and waiting, not rapping his fingers against the arm of the chair, not thumbing through a magazine, not walking around restlessly, nor staring out of the window. He was just sitting in a chair quietly, self-contained. He was so different, Dana thought, admiring him and yet feeling exasperated. She could never figure him out.

"Hey, Shelley," he said pleasantly, rising to greet the girls.

"Hi, Randy," Shelley answered, feeling a little nervous.

Dana plunged right in. "Listen, Randy, I honestly can't get away from that book report tonight but Shelley's dying to see *The Grapes of Wrath* and she'd love to go with you."

"If it's really okay with you, Randy," Shelley said, smiling her bright, open smile. As long as she was being a pal, she'd be a wholehearted one. "I've been wanting to see it and Tom already has — five times. Will you let me go with you?"

"It would be a pleasure," he answered with a warm smile.

Dana was relieved that Randy had been

so charming. If he had seemed annoyed or anything, she knew Shelley would have been embarrassed.

"Have a good time, kids," Dana said, waving them off. "We have our date Sunday, right, Randy? I'll see you then."

In Room 407, Dana felt as though a load had been lifted away and she settled at her desk comfortably to reread and make notes for her book report. When Faith came in a few hours later, she was happily working away.

"Hey," Faith said, "I thought you were going to the movies with Randy."

"Oh, I had to finish this book report. I sent Shelley with him."

Faith raised an eyebrow but didn't say a word. She went to the closet and tossed her coat toward a hook. Sometimes the coats actually landed on the hooks. Faith kicked off her boots, flopped on her bed, and picked up the latest issue of *General Photographer*, her favorite magazine. Sometimes the ways of her roommates mystified her. Faith often thought it was lucky for her that her mother, down there in D.C., was a social worker who had made a point of teaching her children good common sense. Common sense was something Dana didn't seem to have at the moment. *Dana, honey, that's dangerous*, Faith felt like saying to the girl so busy at her desk. But there were times to say things out loud and times not to. The whole Thompson family knew that.

Faith suddenly stopped thinking about Dana. She was back five years at the ceremony honoring her father, her perfect dad, Police Officer Walter Thompson, who "gave his life in heroic performance of duty." That was what the memorial plaque called his being killed stopping a bank robbery. Faith, her older sister Sarah, even her baby brother Richie had learned then, at that ceremony, how sometimes you can't say out loud what you feel.

Dana slapped her book closed. "That's it," she said, and leaned contentedly back in her chair.

Dana, I hope you know what you're doing, Faith thought.

CHAPTER TWO

"Y ou get the Brown Beaver Badge," Shelley said as they left the dorm.

"What's that and why?" Randy asked, smiling.

"For grace under pressure," she said. "At least, I think that's how it goes. It's the way they describe heroes."

"Hey. Nothing heroic about going out with you. It's my pleasure."

"See. That's what I mean."

As they walked in the brisk winter evening toward Randy's pickup truck, neither of them seemed to have much more to say. But after they were in the truck, Randy turned to Shelley and smiled his crooked smile. "I admit this is the first time I ever went out with a girl who was asked to take another girl's place."

"It's sure a first for me, too," Shelley said in a voice that unexpectedly sounded ten times too loud. Hearing herself, Shelley started to giggle. Then, although she had wanted to stay cool and sophisticated about the whole thing, she collapsed in a complete fit of giggles. Randy laughed, too, and laughing together, at ease with each other, they drove into Greenleaf and Randy found a parking spot right across the street from the movie theater.

Afterwards they went to the pizza hangout and talked about the movie over a pizza with all the trimmings. The old black-and-white film was a classic. It depicted farmers from Oklahoma forced to leave their land and become migrant workers, called "Okies," and who traveled West trying to find work during the Depression. Shelley was uncharacteristically somber.

"We have family stories about the Depression," she said, musing, not even biting into the pizza. "My grandfather's brother was an Okie. I guess that's what he was. The Depression wasn't as bad in Iowa as it was in Oklahoma, but even in Iowa, crop prices were just terrible. After four failed crops in five years, he took off from the farm, just ran off and became a hobo."

"Hey, that's interesting. Do you know what happened to him?" Randy asked.

"Oh, he roamed around the country, riding in freight trains, sleeping in hobo jungles, cooking beans in coffee cans. He finally came back to the farm." Shelley smiled as she told this old family story. "But he would never eat beans again, ever, for the rest of his life. And neither would his children."

Randy laughed, but then he, too, spoke seriously. "I can't really imagine the Depression."

"All I know is that it was very tough for farmers," Shelley said. "My great-grandfather was supposed to have said 'The Depression had pups on our doorstep.' He meant they really had to struggle to keep the farm going."

"I don't think it was the same in the East," Randy said. "My great-grandparents probably were losing a lot of their money in the stock market, not in crops. But whenever I want something big, like my truck, or a good stereo . . ." he smiled as he spoke, "my dad is sure to say, 'Did you know that during the Depression a family in Arkansas walked 900 miles to try to find work?' I think he read that once and never forgot it. What he means is that I can have what I want but I have to work for it."

"But Dana says you want to work on your dad's land."

"I do, but I wasn't always as sensible as I am now," Randy answered, smiling his quirky grin.

"Pups-on-the-doorstep is one of our family jokes," Shelley said, smiling in return. "Whenever twenty things go wrong at the same time, my mother, or my father, or my brothers, or somebody's sure to say, 'Let's get those pups off the doorstep.' "

"I guess there were two big things in our ancestors' lives," Randy said. "World War II and before that, the Depression."

"Well, I guess so. Anyway, my father's a pharmacist, not a farmer."

"No more family farm?" asked Randy.

"Oh, sure," Shelley said. "One of my uncles has it."

"We're not primarily farm people," said Randy, stretching his long legs at the side of the booth. "I'm going to be first generation to work the farm full-time."

"Land here isn't like it is at home," Shelley said. It was almost as though she were fingering Massachusetts soil, comparing it with the rich soil of Iowa.

"It's fine for raising horses," Randy said.

They sat eating their pizza in a comfortable silence.

When they were outside again, the black night sky was pierced by what looked like a billion sharp stars.

"Well, there's Orion," Shelley said, looking up. "Hi, Big Bear."

"How do you know such things?" Randy asked, with delight.

"I don't know," she said, "I guess I learned about the stars in the summer." He smiled his laid-back smile as Shelley explained. "On summer nights when I was little and it was very, very hot . . . before we had air condition- ing . . . on some of those hot nights, my father would wake us all up shouting, 'Okay, everybody, we're going out.' I'd be in bed and I'd hear my mother call out, 'Take your sheets, children.' My brothers and I would grab our sheets and we'd all troop downstairs and go outside in our pajamas. . . .''

As she was talking, Shelley had a flash of thought: *If I were telling this to Tom, I'd make a joke of it.*

"We'd lay our sheets out on the lawn and try to go to sleep," she continued. "Of course, it was so much fun we didn't go to sleep right away. So when we were lying there on our backs looking up at the sky, my father would say, 'That's Orion,' and 'That's the Big Dipper.' I guess I learned the names of the constellations without even knowing I was learning them."

Randy practically slapped his hand against his thigh with pleasure. "That's great," he said. "Sleeping out like that. Wow!"

"It *was* pretty great, now that I think about it," Shelley agreed.

"I learned about constellations differently," Randy said. "Hey, did you see that shooting star? I had a book, and my parents gave me a telescope when I was a kid."

As they walked toward Randy's pickup truck, they were both aware of their arms swinging next to each other, not touching. Randy looked at Shelley, a glance out of the corner of his eye at her wide, bright face. There was a big contrast between this bone-deep Midwestern girl and her New York roommate whom he had been dating and liked very much. He decided he liked his girlfriend's roommate, too, but in a completely different way from the way he felt about Dana.

He opened the door on the passenger side of the truck and helped Shelley up the high step into the truck. As he went around to the driver's side, she watched his loping walk that sometimes seemed to bother Dana. It was like back home for Shelley. He settled beside her and fastened the seat belt and shot one of his quirky, nice smiles down at her.

Shelley suddenly found herself busy contrasting Randy with the boys in her life. She compared him to her Greenleaf friend, Tom, who, like her, was deeply interested in theatricals. She thought Tom tossed a long, thin wool scarf around his neck more dramatically than anybody west of the Hudson River. He was a funny, talented East Coast boy who was so different from her that he was like someone from another world, an exotic.

Randy, although he, too, was East Coast, was different in another way. She realized that being with him this evening had been like being with Paul back home. There was something in his way of looking at things that made Shelley feel comfortable. He was like Paul, like all the people she knew in Iowa — except there was something else, something extra. But she wasn't sure yet what it was.

Shelley couldn't remember the last time she

had spoken so honestly about herself and her family as she had this evening with Randy. She wasn't even sure she liked showing the flashes of her deepest seriousness.

As the truck clattered through the dark night back to Canby Hall, Shelley and Randy made silly jokes, laughed, and had a very nice time. When they finally pulled up in front of Baker House, Randy turned around to face Shelley and said, "It's been a great evening. I've felt so easy with you."

"I've felt exactly the same, Randy. It was a real nice evening." She got out of the truck, called out, "See you," and was inside the dormitory before he had time to shift gears and drive off.

Shelley was pensive while she was signing Alison's check-in book for all the girls. If new horizons were to expand for her, as her family expected when they encouraged her to come to Canby Hall, so far from home, well, then, it wasn't such a good idea, was it, to blabber away about these real *home* things, the way she had done with Randy. Such stuff was to save for Paul when she was in Pine Bluff.

That question settled in her mind, Shelley hurried up the stairs and into Room 407. Dana, Faith, Casey, Cheryl Stern, and a couple of other girls were listening to Faith's favorite old Billie Holiday records.

"Hey ho," said Faith as Shelley came in with a hello wave to everybody.

"Well, Dana, I had a good time," Shelley said.

"There, see," Dana said. "The strong, silent type isn't so awful after all."

"Oh, no," Shelley said. "I think your boyfriend's very nice."

"Yes, he is," Dana said, sincerely agreeing with her.

"Swell," Faith said, and went over to change the record.

"Did you *love* the movie?" asked Casey. She was teasing. Over the summer, exposed to theatrical exaggeration almost all day every day for a month, Shelley had discovered the word "love" to describe just about anything — she "loved" the purple felt-tip pen with which she wrote letters to Paul, she "loved" the rip in the corner of the quilt on her bed, she "loved" the way she hated to get up in the morning.

"I absolutely did," Shelley answered. "Henry Fonda was wonderful. Do you remember him, that old actor in *On Golden Pond* and lots of other movies? He played a young Okie during the Depression."

"When was that?" Casey asked.

"I don't know, exactly," Shelley answered. "Fifty, sixty, seventy years ago."

"Ancient history," Cheryl murmured. "Who cares."

The girls concentrated on the great jazz singer singing some of the old-time music that Faith had introduced to her friends.

Shelley hummed and sang along — she had heard the records often enough to learn most of the words but never quite got the rhythm exactly right — until the record was over.

"More," she said.

Faith looked at her watch. "There's supposed to be lights out in about six and a half minutes."

"Does that bother us?" Shelley asked. Somehow she was feeling over-exuberant, over-enthusiastic. "What's in the food locker? Whose blanket do we use to stuff the bottom of the door? Mine, of course."

She stripped the quilt from the top of her bed and rolled it against the bottom of the door so that neither sound nor light could escape into the corridor. They had to be careful. After lights out, they were supposed to be in their individual rooms and lights were supposed to be out.

CHAPTER THREE

Alison's traditional Sunday morning buffet was in full swing. A central table offered pitchers of fruit juice and of milk, an urn of coffee, and heaping plates of doughnuts to all the girls gathered in the lounge. Dana, though, was only having a cup of coffee this morning. She expected Randy to arrive any minute to take her out to the Crowell farm for breakfast, and even a hearty eater like Dana had to prepare for that experience.

"Randy never calls it brunch," she once explained to her roommates, "but that's what it really is, a combination of breakfast out of the old chuck wagon after roundin' up steers since sunup and free lunch at the saloon in a John Wayne movie."

"Sounds delicious," Shelley had said.

"If you're hungry," Faith said. She sort of agreed with Dana. It sounded like too much.

On Sundays, the girls in 407 often stayed
in their room and had a private footlocker
breakfast — leftover pizza, chocolate cookies,
peanut butter, the soft bagels that were Faith's
favorites — but today they had come downstairs because Dana and Faith had early dates
to wait for and Shelley wanted to be sociable.
She also wanted to read the Arts & Leisure
section — the theatrical news section — of the
New York Times, which, like the Boston
paper, came to the dorm every Sunday.

Faith, restless, put down the doughnut she
was nibbling and went over to the enormous,
ornate, art nouveau mirror at the back of the
hallway. There she poked at her trim afro,
smoothed her faded jeans at her lean hips
and down her long legs. She tucked in her
lumberjack wool shirt, pulled it out again,
untied the scarf from her neck, tied it around
her slim waist, paused, moved, paused again
to study the all-over effect.

"You look gorgeous, in case you didn't
know," Dana said, wandering into the hall,
and giving Faith a warm smile.

Dana, whose mother was a buyer at one of
New York's high-style stores, was Room 407's
fashion expert. The *dorm* fashion expert,
everyone reluctantly admitted, was Pamela
Young, whose mother was a famous movie
star and whose clothes ran from terrific to
sensational.

From the depths of one of the large leather

chairs in the lounge, Shelley looked up from the newspaper, caught Faith's eye, and made an approving circle of her thumb and first finger.

Both roommates knew that Johnny was the first boy to make Faith really feel like fussing. Johnny was serious about Faith, too. Proof of that was his ringing the Baker House doorbell exactly at that moment. His date with Faith was just to keep her company while she went wandering around taking pictures for a story for the school paper.

"My friends," Faith said, thanking them with a little nod. She was usually so cool, so laid-back, that to be caught fidgeting slightly embarrassed her.

Johnny's arms were out for her when she opened the door. "My girl," he said happily, and wrapped them around her. Faith hugged him back. There was nothing she could do about it. She liked Johnny Bates. Disentangling herself from him, she kissed him quickly on the cheek, grabbed her jacket, slung her camera over her shoulder, and closed the door behind them.

Promptly at eleven, exactly the time he said he would be there, Randy arrived. When Dana saw him standing on the doorstep — lanky, blond, smiling his slow grin — she felt suddenly shy. Dana always thought of herself as the straight-on type. So did her roommates and her other friends. But lately something about Randy seemed to set her . . . well, at an angle.

"Hi, Randy."

"Hi."

"Want to come in for a cup of coffee?" she asked.

"No, thanks. I think the flapjacks are on already," he answered.

"Okay. I'm ready," Dana said. "My coat's right here."

Good-byes, and they were outside.

No matter how carefully she practiced, Dana never felt she climbed into the passenger seat of Randy's truck with any kind of grace. Maybe you need longer legs, she thought. Maybe it's some sort of country technique you have to be born to. Randy, however, never seemed to notice, or, if he did, it didn't matter to him. Going around to the other side of the truck, climbing in, settling behind the wheel, he tilted his cowboy hat back from his forehead and grinned down at her.

"Glad to be with you, Dana," he said.

Dana squeezed his arm.

"I'm glad to be with you, too, Randy," she said.

And it was true, she realized. Randy was certainly not like the ideal boy she always dreamed of for herself, somebody golden and suave and debonair and witty. Someone like, well, like Michael Frank, the school counselor, but different, younger. Randy's hair was golden, but he was "aw shucks" from the tip of that cowboy hat to the mud-caked heels of his boots. *But*, she thought, *those other things aren't as important as I used to think they were. Randy's terrific, and if I didn't have to prove my devotion to him by having steak for breakfast pretty soon, I'd be almost completely happy this minute.*

The truck took off with a cough and a rattle.

"We just got a new brood mare up from Kentucky," Randy said proudly. "Wait till you see her. She's a beauty."

"I'm looking forward to it."

"Shelley knows more about horses than you do," he said, glancing down at her with a teasing smile.

"Sure she does," said Dana, laughing with him.

"Horses are what I like," he said.

Dana felt put off by his tone, as though he were answering something she hadn't said.

"Shelley said she had a good time with you Friday," she said after a while.

"I did, too. I liked getting to know her better," Randy said.

"Shelley's special," Dana said.

"I believe it. Of course, so's her roommate," Randy said, smiling his quirky smile at Dana.

Dana leaned back against the sheepskin covering of the seats of the truck. "Thanks for the kind words," she said. Randy *was* kind; that was a large part of why she liked him so much, why she wanted so much to restore the faith and trust that he had had in her and that she had shattered so casually when she met Michael. Her feeling for Randy was not love, but it was special and good; he was very important to her.

"Okay, Randy, now listen. I want to hear about the mare. Tell me about it," she said.

"A mare's a *her*."

Dana laughed. "I'll learn. Tell me about *her*," she said. As he talked, Dana looked through the truck window. She watched the town of Greenleaf become country with wide fields marked by an occasional high red silo, a neat white farm house, land divided by low old stone walls into patches of different shades of stubble tan and earth brown, cows grazing, horses loping, an occasional group of goats or sheep. Soon they were riding by the split-rail fencing that marked the Crowell farm. The fencing went along the road as far as the eye could see, and after that, it curved inward for many acres, Dana knew. At different times, she had gone with Randy and one or another of his five brothers when they drove out to examine or repair the fencing. The fences went past the Crowell apple orchards, around the corral, along the far borders of the pasture.

Randy turned the truck into the tree-lined entrance road and drove up to the house. Dana was always surprised that this neat, white house looked so small when it was really big, and easily held the large and vigorous Crowell family, all the brothers and Randy's father and mother.

Soon everyone was seated around the enormous table in the oversized kitchen. It was a long, marble-topped table, and the kitchen was as large, Dana thought, as her whole living room in the apartment in New York. She felt a little overwhelmed at the number of people — six men, two women — around that table, and by the noise level! Maybe Randy had become so quiet as protection against the volume of sound of his brothers, and of his mother and father, too.

"More flapjacks, Dana?" called out Mr. Crowell, who was at the enormous griddle.

Dana didn't understand why, although she enjoyed the high spirits and activity of the table, she felt peculiar, nervous. She looked down at her plate and once again — it happened every time she sat at this table — she wasn't hungry, could barely pick at the flapjacks, the steak, the fried potatoes, the tomatoes, the eggs, the muffins, the pies.

Suddenly she had a thought. She realized that before she came away from home, here, to Canby Hall, she and her mother and her sister seldom sat down to this kind of a meal together. They fixed themselves quick things for breakfast and often ate quickly, too — laughing and together but on the run. Dinners often depended on everyone's different sched-

ules, Maggie's and hers at school, her mother's
at the store where she was a buyer. But the
biggest difference between her family and
Randy's family, thought Dana, looking up
and down the long table, was that when hers
sat down, they were only three people. Dana
felt a pang of longing for her father, so
happily married now to Eve. She couldn't
remember anymore what it was like when
her father was at the table with them.

". . . so as soon as you're ready, we'll go. . . .
Dana. Dana?" It was Randy speaking. Dana
realized she had slipped away, had been lost
in her thoughts, didn't know what they were
talking about.

Soon she knew. She and Randy and two of
his brothers — talkative Bob, whom she knew
well, and Teddy, who was even quieter than
Randy — were driving to the stables in the
pickup truck. The dog was in the front seat
between her and Randy. He wagged his big
collie tail in Dana's face as he poked his head
happily out the window.

Dana was impressed again, as she had been
the first time Randy brought her to his
family's farm, by how neat and cared-for
everything looked. Randy stooped to pick up
a scrap of paper that blew against his foot as
they walked toward the stable and dropped
the paper into a wastebasket standing at the
entrance.

"Here she is," he said, stopping at one of the stalls in which there was a horse that looked to Dana pretty much like any black horse. Dana instinctively drew back as Randy called, and the horse turned and thrust her big head out of the stall, toward them.

"Don't be afraid," Randy said gently. Dana couldn't really tell whether he was talking to her or the horse.

Dana reached a tentative hand out to touch the big head, the soft nose. Randy took the hand in his own and Dana was sure he was going to bend down and kiss her right then and there. Instead, he placed a cube of sugar in her palm. Of course he couldn't kiss her here, she thought. They were too public, with Bob and Teddy in the stable, too.

"Hold your hand flat out to her," Randy said. Dana did, felt the sensation of the horse's velvety mouth scoop up the sugar, and then didn't know what to do about the slather on her hand. She didn't really want to rub it off against her jeans, her best jeans that had come out of the laundry machine only yesterday.

"I won't give you a lesson in raising horses," he promised.

Dana smiled her appreciation but noticed the proud expression on his face as he led the horse out of the stall, ran a hand down its back, along a leg, pulled at its mane and exchanged opinions with his brothers about configuration and freshness and other things she didn't begin to understand.

"I guess more than anything else, Randy wanted to show me this new brood mare they just got from some horse place in Kentucky," Dana reported to her roommates that evening. "It was a beautiful horse," she said. She pushed her hair back, tucked it behind her ears. "He's really interested in horses," she said.

"But that's what he wants to do for the rest of his life, breed horses," Shelley said.

"I know. It's wonderful. Terrific. He's a wonderful guy," Dana said, suddenly ready to change the subject. *How*, she asked herself, *can you, Dana Morrison, 100 percent city girl, be tangled up with a boy whose aim in life is horses? How can it be that you like him so much, anyhow?!*

"I have a compliment for you, Shel," she said. "He thinks you're great."

"That's good. It makes us even," Shelley said, pulling a flowered flannel nightgown over her head. "Did you tell him I said he was nice?"

"Sure. Have to have my friends liking each other," Dana said.

CHAPTER FOUR

"It was beautiful in the woods yesterday," Faith said as she, Dana, Shelley, and some other girls walked, shivering, across campus to Main Building for first period Monday morning. "There were all those last autumn leaves on the ground and the trees were finally bare. It was great for pictures. I even got Johnny to pose with the lioness."

The girls laughed. They did not always show the greatest respect for their school emblem, a lioness, nor for its representative, a weathered old bronze statue of a lioness with her cubs that stood on a stone base in the grove of birch trees.

"What can I say?" Faith said, laughing, shrugging. "I'm doing a picture story about the traditions and symbols of Canby Hall."

Pamela Young, walking by with her loyal hangers-on, Ellie Bolton and Mary Beth Grover, heard the laughing and smiled one of her icy, nasty smiles. "Isn't laughter and friendship really wonderful?" she said sarcastically.

"What's that supposed to mean?" Faith asked.

"Don't ask me to tell you, darling. Some people really live in a fool's paradise," Pamela answered with her tinkling little laugh. Her friends dutifully reacted with her. Ellie, a self-possessed junior, possibly a little embarrassed to be hanging around with Pamela, simply rolled her eyes skyward but Mary Beth, more eager, an awkward. sophomore who tagged after Pamela in the sad hope that some of Pamela's glamor might brush off on her, practically snorted. The three of them quickly moved ahead, Pamela smiling her icy, tight smile and pointing her beautiful chin into the air.

Shelley stuck her thumbs in her ears, wiggled her fingers and crossed her eyes behind them.

"Magic doesn't work on her, Shel," Faith said, almost gritting her teeth.

"Pamela Young brings out my ten worst sides," Dana said. "Also, I would kill for those boots she's wearing."

Pamela was perhaps the least-liked girl in Baker House. Almost more beautiful than her famous mother, she had made a monumental stir when she first arrived at Canby Hall the year before. Girls watching from the windows and in the halls of the dorm had taken it in good spirit when she was driven to the door in a chauffeured limousine, emerged like a princess, and made her entrance loaded down with trunks, bags, a stereo, three tennis racquets, skis, a camera that had made Faith drool — for an instant — and a mink coat.

Everybody was ready to like her but Pamela instantly made herself disliked. She originally turned off Faith and Dana by being condescending to the one and rude to the other. It had taken stagestruck Shelley a little while longer to realize that no number of stories about the famous theatrical people she knew made up for Pamela's nastiness. Girls learned to be on their guard when she laughed her tinkling laugh and to look for the barb in everything she said.

"What's with the wicked witch from the West Coast?" asked Casey who was ambling along with Faith.

"Who cares?" Dana said. She was trying to figure out if she could squeeze an hour for jogging into her busy day. Today she had Choral Club after classes and she wasn't sure she could get back to Baker House to change to her running shoes before Choral began.

Once inside Main Building, the group split up, Shelley heading upstairs to Medieval History and the others around the corner to English 3: Introduction to Shakespeare.

* * *

There were blue answer books on every desk.

"Oh, joy," Casey exclaimed when she saw them. "Monday's starting with a test."

"Not to worry," Dana said. Then she saw the blank blackboard and the clean top of Ms. MacPherson's desk. "Whoops, I take it back," she said. "You can worry. No stack of xeroxed question sheets, nothing written on the blackboard. It's going to be one of her cute ones."

Casey groaned and sank dramatically into her chair.

Pamela, at her desk, carefully adjusted the sleeves of her stunning beige cashmere sweater and leaned across the aisle toward Dana. "I thought you might be interested, Dana," she said in her most sugary voice, "in an observation I made over the weekend."

"Not really," Dana said, carefully offhanded but putting herself immediately on guard. Pamela's malice could be wildly imaginative.

"Well, you should be," Pamela said spitefully. "I was at Pizza Pete's last Friday, and I saw your roommate and your boyfriend there. Together."

So that was the big number! Dana tried to keep her face straight. Pamela was working hard to make trouble and there wasn't anything to work on. "That's nice," Dana said smiling.

"You know who I mean, don't you? Good-looking Randy. And innocent little Shelley."

"Sure," Dana said.

"They seemed to be utterly entranced with each other."

"Okay, m'dears." Ms. MacPherson's voice was crisp and clear. "As you can see, I've put out blue books for a test. Be careful, take your time, because there's only one question and this is the only test you'll be having on *Macbeth*." Ms. MacPherson didn't pause. "And Pamela, will you let all of us in on your important conversation?"

Pamela was startled. "I beg your pardon, Ms. MacPherson?"

"I asked you to stop talking, Pamela. The class started quite a while ago."

"I'm sorry."

"I also asked you to let us all know what you were so busy saying."

Every head in the room swiveled in their direction as Pamela glanced at Dana and stood up with a flourish and a smirk.

Dana sat back and waited. "She's going to made a dope of herself for a change," she whispered to Casey who sat at the desk behind hers.

"Of course, Ms. MacPherson," Pamela said. She didn't seem the slightest bit embarrassed. She didn't even have to clear her throat. "I was just telling Dana that I saw her boyfriend in Greenleaf with her roommate this weekend," Pamela said.

A big "Wow!" resounded through the room and all heads swiveled from Pamela to Dana.

"Happy day," Faith murmured.

Dana felt her cheeks getting redder and redder. Shelley was the constant blusher of the roommates, but at this moment, cool Dana's face was scarlet. What's more, she felt suddenly as if there really was something wrong. The way Pamela said it, Shelley out with Randy did sound awful.

"Okay. Simmer down," Ms. MacPherson said.

Dana quickly stood up. "May I please tell the rest of it? I want to say that everybody, anybody, could have seen Randy and Shelley last Friday. It was perfectly all right that they were together. It was my idea. I *asked* Shelley to go out with him."

To Dana's astonishment, everybody laughed.

"I *did*," Dana insisted, turning to one side, then the other, then to Ms. MacPherson. "If Shelley were here, she'd tell you the same thing."

"I just bet," Pamela said with her tinkling laugh. Loud laughter and a buzz rolled around the room as heads clustered together and giggles rose and subsided into whispers.

As Dana sat down, she realized that nobody believed her.

"It's not fair," Casey said, leaning forward over her desk and whispering into the back of Dana's ear. Dana shrugged, too surprised and shocked to say anything.

"Here's the test," Ms. MacPherson said sharply. "Pick out something interesting in *Macbeth* and write an essay about it. That's the whole thing. You can use the textbook as much as you want to. You have the rest of the hour."

"Not fair!" Casey said again, and this time there was a new intensity in her whisper. " 'Pick out something interesting and write an essay about it.' Crazy!" Casey liked true-or-false questions. She always had trouble organizing her thoughts into essays. "Would you believe she's calling that a real test? It'll affect grades!"

Dana didn't answer. She was still shaken by the way the class had taken Pamela's word against hers.

Casey bit the end of her pencil. "I don't remember anything," she said with a groan. "This is the play about the prince of Denmark, right?"

Dana made a sympathetic sound just loud enough for Casey to hear and then bit the end of her own pencil. She knew the assignment was trickier than it seemed, and she could not concentrate. They had been studying *Macbeth* for a week. There were dozens of "something interesting"s to choose. Finding one with a theme to write about — that was the challenge, that was what made you think.

But as she leafed through the text of the

play, all Dana could think about was Pamela's smirking face and how everybody had laughed at her, Dana, when she told the simple truth about Shelley's going out with Randy. She almost couldn't catch her breath, as though she had had a physical blow. How could anybody like being nasty, the way Pamela did? Pamela had loved standing up there. Maybe she had hoped Ms. MacPherson would catch her and make her say her little piece out loud.

From behind her, Dana could hear Casey, still muttering, but working, turning the pages of her answer book.

Never mind Pamela. Concentrate on the test, Dana told herself.

Looking down at the book, she saw the words "Out, out damned spot!" It was the beginning of Lady Macbeth's famous sleep-walking speech in *Macbeth*, where she tries to wash away the blood she imagined was on her hands because she had made her husband commit murder. *Out, Pamela!* Dana thought, and that gave her an idea for her essay: cruel people like Lady Macbeth and Pamela Young can't ever wash away their sins.

Struggling with the theme that she knew was too complicated — and personal — to turn out right, Dana didn't notice the increased muttering behind her. But Casey's other neighbors did.

"Shush, Casey."

"Quiet, *puh*-leeze."

"That's enough, Casey," said the strong and

commanding voice of Ms. MacPherson, the school's dramatics teacher, who had been an actress once. Casey coughed and went on scribbling in her blue book. That was one of her old ways, not to look up but to cough and muffle the troublemaking things she felt like saying or doing. It meant that Casey was scared.

The bell finally rang.

"Come on, kids," Faith said, coming over to Dana and Casey and putting an arm around each of them. "Never mind Pamela," she said to her roommate, "and never mind unexpected tests," she said to Casey. "Not everybody is as sweet as we are. Now, who wants to go into Greenleaf after classes this afternoon and do some serious shopping for a sweater? Winter is a' comin' and I was thinking, I'd love to find a blue cardigan with big, puffy shoulders."

"Can't today. I've got Choral," Dana said.

"I can," Casey said. Faith glanced quickly at her mercurial friend.

"Great," Faith said. "Three o'clock in the Student Lounge?"

"Correct," said Casey. "In time for *As the World Spins*." There was no reason why they shouldn't see their favorite soap opera before they left.

"Are you all right, Dana?" Faith asked as the two of them walked out of the room and down the hall together.

"Sure. Well, I mean, I guess I'm really not.

I . . . I'm not used to people laughing at me. Why did they laugh? I told the truth. Why didn't they believe me?"

"What can I say?"

"I've never been humiliated like that, Faith."

"It'll blow over, I promise. Pretty soon everybody'll figure out that anything that sounds so wild has to be true," Faith said.

She patted her roommate's arm encouragingly. "Sorry you can't come with Casey and me, Dana. It might make you feel better."

"Yeah. I know."

The town of Greenleaf was something like the safety valve of Canby Hall. When life within the school gates seemed a little tight, the small New England town, which was a long walk, a shorter bike ride, and an even shorter bus trip away, gave the girls a sense of freedom. They went to the Tutti-Frutti for restorative ice cream sundaes or Pizza Pete's for elaborate pizzas that could turn supper into something more fun than the school dining hall. Sometimes a girl carried a pizza back to her dorm where she and her chums ate it, cold but delicious, at their sloppy ease.

The supermarket in town was the source of Band-aids, notebooks with rock star pictures on the glossy covers, sewing supplies, toys and funny things to put up on their walls, and almost all of the essential supplies of food they kept in their rooms.

Teen Togs was for new jeans when their jeans became too tattered to pass the dress code and The Fancy Dress Shop was just right for two girls who were upset, one because her roommate seemed unhappy and the other because of an unexpected English test. After Faith and Casey spent two and a half hours that afternoon looking at and trying on sweaters, coats, skirts, and pretty dresses, they both felt terrific when they got on the bus back to school, and Faith had a box under her arm.

CHAPTER FIVE

Tom's motorcycle roared to a stop and Shelley, huddled behind him as much for warmth as for safety, loosened her arms from his waist and looked around at Waterville, two towns past Greenleaf. It was ten in the morning and the pretty New England town shimmered in the hard, winter morning light.

"This is where I leave you, Shel," Tom said. He was going miles further, to the outskirts of Boston.

Shelley unhooked her helmet and got off the motorcycle. "Do you know where the library is?" she asked.

"Sure. Right in front of you," he said, pointing to a weather-beaten white clapboard house.

"Is that a *library*?"

"It's what they call a charming New England library, Shelley." Tom fastened the helmet Shelley had been wearing to its special place on the motorcycle, took his own helmet off, and rubbed his hand through his hair. "I wish I could stay with you."

"I wish you could, too," Shelley said.

In order for Shelley to go on this expedition, she had had to get special permission, not just because she was skipping two classes but also because a Canby Hall girl was not supposed to go further than Greenleaf — was not really supposed even to go to Greenleaf — without being with another Canby Hall girl. "I prefer two girls to go together," Miss Allardyce always said when she explained the rule at the start of every school year. For Tom to take her had required even more special permission. Now Tom was leaving.

"Don't worry, Tom," Shelley said.

"You going to take the noon bus back?"

"Sure," Shelley said. "I'm just going to get the book they're holding for me and catch the bus. I'll be back at school before lunch break is over."

"Well, if you miss the one at noon, the next one is at four-thirty," he said. "That'd get you back to Canby Hall so late you'd never be able to get out again — and I would never more see you in this sweet life."

Tom, like Shelley, could be very theatrical. He tossed his long, thin, wool scarf over his shoulder in the way that always made Shelley melt.

"Don't worry, Tom," she said, and leaned

over and kissed him on the end of his nose.
Then she put her arms around him and
hugged him with great enthusiasm. "Oh, I
love hugging you in public in a strange town,"
she exclaimed.

Tom disentangled himself. "Shel, I want
you to do something for me."

"Anything, Tom," Shelley answered.

"Save me the first dance Saturday night."

With that, he put on and fastened his
helmet, started the motorcycle, fed it gas so it
roared, and was away, the scarf flying behind
him. Shelley grinned and waved at him. There
wasn't a dance or a party on Saturday. He
was being Tom, asking for a date.

"Your library system certainly is wonderful," Shelley said, smiling her wide Iowa smile
as the Waterville librarian found the book
that had been reserved in her name and
checked it out to her. "Our school library
didn't have the book I wanted, and they got
in touch with the Greenleaf library and they
didn't have it, and they got in touch with you
and you had it and you held it for me and now
I have it. I absolutely love the way that
happened."

"I'm glad we could help you," said the
librarian, responding to Shelley's exuberance.

Shelley looked at her watch. It was only
quarter to eleven. She had lots of time before
the noon bus.

I'll poke around the library, she decided. It was pretty inside as well as out, worn old oak bookshelves — but microfilm shelves, too, she noticed, and machines to read microfilm on — and a whole big theater section.

Funny they should have so many theater books, she said to herself, leafing through one called *At 33*. It was the autobiography of an old, interesting actress named Eva Le Gallienne. Then she picked up another autobiography, *Past Indicative*, written by one of Tom's favorite all-around theater men, Noel Coward. She was ready to sit down with both books when she heard someone say her name.

"Shelley? It can't be Shelley. Wrong time, wrong place."

She looked up into the laughing eyes of Randy Crowell.

"What are you doing here?" They both asked the question at the same time.

"You first," said Shelley, returning the books to the shelf and giving her whole attention to Randy.

"I come for barbed wire," he said.

"To the library?" Shelley asked with an innocent expression. Shelley could no more help flirting with a boy — which is what that was — than she could help having blue eyes and curly blonde hair.

"Hey," Randy said. "No, I get barbed wire over at Hawkins' and then I come here and get myself a supply of reading material. How about you? What brings you so far from home territory? Aren't you supposed to be in school?"

"I'm taking some time off," Shelley said, twirling a curl of hair around her finger.

"I recognize that hair-twirling. Doesn't it mean you're doing something you're not supposed to?"

Shelley had the good grace to blush. She really wasn't supposed to be in Waterville alone.

"Look here," Randy said. "It's a little after twelve o'clock, time for lunch. Why don't you and I. . . ."

Shelley almost screeched. "*After* twelve! It can't be. I have to be on the twelve o'clock bus to Greenleaf, and school. If I miss it, I'll probably be expelled."

"I think you *have* missed it, Shelley. In fact, I know you have. The bus was going by as I came in," Randy said.

Shelley bit her lip. "This is almost serious. I really wanted to catch that bus," she said.

"I have my truck. I'll take you back. No problem."

"Okay. You're on," Shelley said.

"*Now* can we have lunch?"

By the time they deposited Shelley's book in Randy's truck and were in a coffee shop halfway through hamburgers, shakes, and french fries, with fried onion rings for good

measure, Shelley's customary good spirits re-
appeared.

"You know what? It's terrific not being in
school on a school day," she said.

Randy leaned back, his thin, beautiful face
lit by a bemused smile. Shelley waited
patiently, watching him, her own smile widen-
ing as the moments passed. Finally she
laughed.

"Aren't you going to say anything?" she
asked.

Randy shook away the cobwebs.

"How'd it happen? How come you're here?"

Shelley explained about the book and the
libraries.

There was another long pause. "I enjoyed
the other evening with you a lot, Shelley,"
he said, "and I'm glad to see you now."

Shelley slowly bit into the french fry she
was holding. This was Randy, Dana's boyfriend. But there was nothing to be concerned
about. "Me, too, Randy," she said gaily.

Sometime after that and before they started
strolling through Waterville as though they
had planned it, Shelley excused herself to call
Alison. She was apologetic. "I missed the bus
so I'll be back late. I wanted you to know."
With that out of the way, she turned her total
attention to Randy.

"Want to go sight-seeing?" he asked.

"Don't you have to get back? Don't you
have chores?"

"Nothing I can't do later. How about I show you an old inn where there's been an inn on the same spot since 1773?"

"Love to," Shelley said.

They walked down the main street of the charming New England town, all white clapboard and wooden fences and old-fashioned storefronts.

"Houses like that, and the picket fences remind me of Iowa. But why does the place look so — well, picture-book?" Shelley asked. "Where're the supermarkets and the laundry places, places like that?"

"They're here, but they're disguised," Randy said. "In the summer, Waterville's a tourist hangout."

"Oh," Shelley said.

"Here's the inn I was telling you about," he said, stopping in front of a rambling, colonial-looking inn with rocking chairs lined up on its tremendous wooden porch.

"Our house at home has a front porch, too," Shelley said. "And we have the same kind of rocking chairs."

"Back in the 1700s, stagecoaches used to stop here. To and from Boston," Randy said. "Once there was a convention here to protest the taxes on imports from England. Boston Tea Party stuff."

"I didn't know you were a history buff," Shelley said.

"Well, when you come from a place, you grow up automatically knowing this kind of thing." He paused, and his slow smile crept across his face.

"Why're you smiling?" Shelley asked.

"Oh, the man who owns this place plays Santa Claus on Christmas. He walks up and down the main street in a red suit and a white beard, calling out ho ho ho."

"That's cute," Shelley said.

"Come on, I want you to see something in the lobby."

They went up the wood steps, crossed the porch, and entered the large, round lobby that reminded Shelley somehow of Baker House, the oldest dorm at Canby Hall. There, standing by the far wall, near the entrance to the dining room of the inn, was a sculpture of a colonial woman — "In honor of Thanksgiving," Randy explained — entirely made of candy.

"This is crazy!" Shelley exclaimed with delight, walking around it. "Gumdrops, and chocolate wafers, and. . . . You know what? It looks good enough to eat." Randy burst out laughing.

"Thank you, Randy Crowell," Shelley said. "I make these terrible jokes all the time and I'm usually the only one who laughs at them."

"That was funny," Randy said.

"Dana says I should save my jokes for Iowa."

The mention of Dana, and in that particular way, instantly dampened their spirits. Dana had been their unacknowledged companion all afternoon. Now her name had been spoken and the atmosphere between them changed.

"This has been fun, Randy," Shelley said formally. "I have to go back now."

Randy tilted his head in acknowledgment.

"Yes, and . . ." she looked at her watch. "It's four-fifteen. I can make the four-thirty bus."

"I'll take you back to Canby Hall, Shelley," Randy said.

"I don't want you to drive me to school, Randy. I'll take the bus," she said.

"That's ridiculous. I want to take you back. For three reasons. It's getting late. That's one reason. I said I would. That's another."

As they walked down the steps of the inn, onto the sidewalk, over toward his pickup truck, he took her hand.

"And here's the third," he said.

Shelley knew she should pull away but she didn't want to. She wanted his work-toughened hand to go on holding hers so gently, so surely.

"The third reason is that I want to be with you as long as possible," Randy said. With that, he bent over, lifted her chin, and lightly kissed her.

"Oh."

Shelley knew she was slipping into a situation that was completely, thoroughly wrong — and yet was almost irresistible to her. It wasn't just that she felt herself responding to Randy's words. She knew that there was also something about Randy, the farm boy from Massachusetts, that appealed deeply to her, the girl from rural Iowa. She tried desperately to fight her feelings.

"Randy, Dana's my roommate," she said earnestly. "She's one of my very closest friends. You're her boyfriend. You really shouldn't say things like that to me."

"I'm not married to Dana," Randy said soberly. "She would be the first to tell you that. I like her a lot. I like you, too. I know I want to see you again."

"I can't say I don't like you, Randy. That wouldn't be honest."

"If you want me to, I'll tell Dana about today."

"Oh, no!" Shelley exclaimed.

"Or we can tell her together."

"No," Shelley said again.

There was a pause. "I don't think we have to say anything, Shelley."

Shelley took a deep breath. "Okay," she said.

They drove slowly through the early dusk in a thought-filled silence until they reached the outskirts of Greenleaf.

"I'll get out here, Randy. I don't want you to drive me further," she said. "Please."

By now it was really dark and Randy insisted. Finally he suggested a compromise.

"I'll leave you outside the gates. Okay?"

Shelley suddenly shook her head hard. "Randy, I hate being sneaky!"

"It'll be all right," he assured her.

Outside the gates, about ten feet from the big, wrought iron gates, he stopped the truck and turned to her. Shelley couldn't help herself, she found herself melting. Like the first time, at the movies, being with him was as comfortable, as easy, as *right* as being with a boy back home. When Randy kissed her, again lightly, she found herself putting her arms around his neck and kissing him back.

"I'll call you, Shelley," he said softly as he reached across her and opened the door of the truck.

Shelley didn't answer. Instead, she waved without turning around and trudged through the gates and down the road to Baker House. She hoped desperately that she would be strong enough not to see him again.

When she got in the dorm and upstairs, she went in and out of Room 407 so fast her roommates hardly saw her. She simply grabbed a towel and fled to the bathroom. There, even though she hadn't had dinner and the dining hall would close in about fifteen minutes, she took a leisurely, hot bath, thinking and soaking, soaking and thinking. It had been a perfect day, there was no way she could tell herself different. And when a boy likes a girl, and tells her so as sweetly as Randy did. . . .

But she couldn't hurt Dana, she couldn't do something so wrong.

After a long time, with nothing resolved in her head, Shelley staggered from the tub to the room, seemingly so exhausted she couldn't even chat it up with her roommates, could only collapse into bed and fall right asleep.

"Hey, don't you have some French that's supposed to be ready tomorrow and weren't you going to do it tonight?" Dana asked. Ever since Shelley almost flunked French a few semesters back, her roommates had taken it on themselves to monitor her.

"S'aw'right. 'll do d'all durin' lunch. Got'l third period 't do'd'all," Shelley mumbled as though she really were almost asleep.

As she huddled under the blankets, eyes closed, Shelley told herself that it was an accidental one-day thing, that nothing was going to happen, that she and Dana's boyfriend became friends today and that was all.

She burrowed her face still deeper into the bed coverings, covered her face entirely, as she tried to decide what she would say if — no, not if, *when* — Randy called her for a date. Then she tried to decide *exactly* what she would say if — no, not if. . . .

Shelley turned, burrowed her face still deeper into the bed coverings, covered her face entirely in order to hide, even from herself, the guilt and embarrassment surging through her. She wasn't sure what she would say when Randy called.

CHAPTER SIX

Although it happened less than a week later, Shelley never found out what she would say when Randy called her. The very first time he tried, Dana answered the phone.

"Baker House," she said.

"Hello. May I speak to —"

"Hey, Randy." Dana recognized his voice instantly. "I must have known you were calling me. I just happened to be passing the phone booths."

"Hi, Dana, honey," Randy said after a second. "How y'doing?"

"Okay. We're having a time with Shelley but other than that. . . .

"What's the matter?" Randy said casually.

Dana laughed. "We don't have conversations anymore. Faith and I are starting *Romeo and Juliet* in English next week and Shelley's preparing us. She recites *Romeo and Juliet* speeches to us all the time."

Unknown to Dana, Randy, at the other end of the phone, grinned. Like everyone else, he knew about Shelley's interest in the theater. What's more, on their day in Waterville, she had told him that, last summer, in the Scenes from Shakespeare workshop she took, *Romeo and Juliet* had been her favorite play.

"Doesn't sound too serious," he said.

"Of course it's not. Shelley really knows her theater stuff. I admire her."

"Me, too," Randy said.

Dana went on to other things. "Listen, Randy. There's going to be a party here a week from Saturday. After my Choral concert, remember?"

"Sure. That's when you're going to be singing music without a tune."

Dana tried to laugh. "Well, sort of," she said. "Music from the Middle Ages. They call it polyphony."

"I don't know about the concert, Dana."

"Like the commercial says, Randy, try it. You'll like it."

"I don't know," he said again.

"They rode horses in the Middle Ages, Randy. Does that tempt you?" Dana said.

"Cut it out, Dana," Randy said.

"I'm sorry," she said quickly. "Please forgive me. I was trying to make a joke but it wasn't funny. The thing is," she hurried on, "after the concert we're giving a party. In the Student Lounge. Take one, you get two. Come to the concert with Faith and Johnny and

Shelley and Tom and then I meet you afterwards, at the party."

"Well. . . ."

Dana took a breath before speaking. "Randy, if you want to, you can skip the concert."

"I just don't know about that kind of music, Dana."

Why doesn't he take a chance? she thought, irritated. He'll never know about "that kind of music" if he won't even listen to it.

"Well, I hope you'll come to the party." Dana began to be irritated. She liked going out with Randy. He was very special to her. Why did she get these flashes of real annoyance because he didn't enjoy something she happened to enjoy?

"I'll be there, Dana. Thanks for asking me. I'll try to come to the concert, too."

"Terrific," Dana said.

"Meanwhile, how about this Saturday? Movies? Pizza?"

"Also terrific."

"No book reports?" he asked.

"No book reports, Randy, I promise," Dana said. As she hung up, Dana felt vaguely, indefinably unhappy. *Sometimes I'm kind of rough on Randy,* she thought, and made a resolution: From now on, nice! But the indefinable something still bothered her as she went slowly up the stairs to the start of Study Hours.

* * *

That Saturday, it seemed as though the whole of Canby Hall was on the line outside the Greenleaf Cinema, in the glistening evening. Never mind the rain. Standing in line outside the Cinema was as much a part of going to the movies as being inside watching the picture. Faith and Johnny, Dana and Randy, had had a pizza supper together — it was a last-minute double-date decision after the girls saw the dinner menu in the dining hall — and now they were bunched together, small-talking, sticking their tongues out to catch raindrops, discussing Michael Jackson and punk hair styles.

"Let's try it," Dana said. "You guys go mohawk and Faith and I will dye pink streaks in our hair. And what do we need to make it stand up in spikes?"

"Elmer's glue?" Faith suggested.

They all laughed and Randy smiled his laid-back smile. "Can we put it off until tomorrow, Dana?"

There was a sudden stir, a rustle, whistles, and applause from further down the line. Johnny stepped out to see what was happening.

"Hey, it's Tom and Shelley," he said.

They all stepped out of line to peer. In the middle of the sidewalk, in the steady rain, Tom was standing, draped in a poncho, wearing a terribly matted red wool wig on his head, his face painted clown-white with a big smile, a red cut-out Ping-Pong ball stuck onto his nose. With everybody's loud encouragement, he was trying to juggle three small, wet, red balls. He was tossing them with great bravado but wasn't catching them very well. The balls kept slipping out of his hands and scudding along the sidewalk.

"It's too wet out," Randy said.

"Or poor Tom doesn't know how to juggle," Dana added. "And look at Shel."

Around, behind, and in front of Tom, Shelley, with all the aplomb of a magician's assistant, was scurrying after the balls as Tom dropped them. Each time she retrieved a ball, she held it up in triumph and handed it back to Tom with a flourish. She, and everyone watching, was having a great time.

"She was telling me about buskers this morning. That's the English word for street performers," Faith said with a loving headshake.

Dana turned to share a smile with Randy, who had pulled back. Randy was so square about so many things, she wasn't sure he would find her roommate and Tom acting like buskers as much fun as the rest of them did. Randy was watching so intently that she couldn't catch his eye. Dana was surprised but pleased that he seemed to be enjoying it all.

Tom and Shelley worked their way up the line. Soon they were opposite their friends who gaily cheered for them. Tom held his hand up.

"Please, no more applause," he said. "No more."

They all laughed and as Shelley did, her eyes and Randy's met and held. But it was only for a moment.

Tom pulled off his wig and shook it out in front of him and voices squealed at the extra sprinkling. Then he took the Ping-Pong ball off his nose — "I made that," Shelley said, "nail polish and my best scissors!" — and put it and the three small juggling balls into the pocket of his jacket.

"I'm ready to quit now," he said ruefully. "I think I need more practice."

When the doors of the theater opened, Johnny linked arms with Faith on one side and Shelley on the other. "Here we go," he said, and started to march forward.

"No." To Johnny's surprise, Shelley tried to pull away. "We were just taking a break."

"Not me, darling," Tom said. "I'm finished."

"But you can't go in there with all that gook on your face."

"My beautiful clown makeup? Sure I can," Tom said, and hooked his arm through Dana's as the line moved forward. Shelley felt uncomfortable. The roommates were now on a triple date.

"I didn't plan this," Shelley managed to whisper to Randy.

"I know. It's okay."

As things worked out, they got six seats together without any trouble. Faith and Johnny, first down the aisle, went first into the row, Dana followed automatically and Randy followed Dana. Shelley and Tom, in that order, had to follow them. Shelley was aware every instant that she was sitting next to Randy.

In the bustle and movement of everybody's unzipping and getting out of wet coats and stuffing them over the seats and offering the popcorn around, Shelley thought she felt Randy touch her knee gently — she wasn't completely sure. She hoped not. She hoped so. Shelley looked over at Tom. His clown white-face was almost glowing in the dark and she thought, *I love you, Tom.* Tom represented fun and excitement and the theater, new attitudes, new ideas, nothing that was anything like Iowa, the life she came from. Randy, though — and she glanced at him out of the corner of her eye — seemed to be a blend of her old world and new one, a wonderful new friend to have. Dana's Randy.

Shelley didn't know where her feelings were taking her, what would happen, how this would end. She hoped none of them — Dana, Randy, or she herself — were going to be hurt.

CHAPTER SEVEN

Ms. MacPherson tapped the stack of blue books against her hand.

"Well, before we get to *Romeo and Juliet*, I'm going to return your *Macbeth* essay tests. I know you thought I had forgotten about them but not so. I read them slowly and carefully because this was an important test. And it was tough, too. . . ."

Ms. MacPherson, a tall, angular, older woman with frizzy red hair, settled herself on the corner of her desk.

". . . very tough because you had to make *one* choice when there were a lot to choose from and on top of that you had to justify your choice. Most of you handled it very well. There's some good thinking and good writing going on in here."

"Somebody has to tell her she talks too much," Casey said to Dana without moving her lips, one of Casey's expert tricks.

Ms. MacPherson started walking up and down the aisles handing out the bluebooks. Little noises followed in her wake — tiny groans, gasps, squeals of pleasure. Dana shrugged at her B minus. It was better than she expected. "Let's talk about this after class," Ms. MacPherson said when she got to Casey.

"No, thanks," Casey answered abruptly.

The whole room went silent.

"Then come tomorrow, Casey. Four o'clock. In my office," Ms. MacPherson said.

Casey — and everyone else who heard it — recognized Ms. MacPherson's quiet request as a command.

"Sure," Casey said in a tough voice.

Dana, right in front of her, heard the voice and was concerned. It sounded as though Casey had bombed on the test and was thrown by it. When Casey put on an I-don't-care act, it meant she was upset and scared.

"What'd ya get, Casey?" Dana whispered after Ms. MacPherson walked on.

"F, rotten F. I flunked." Casey spit the words out.

Dana looked across the room to Faith, who flashed her a grin. English was Faith's one problem subject and the grin meant she had done all right. Dana moved her head back slightly, to indicate Casey, and, raising her hands just high enough for Faith to see, made a circle with the thumb and first finger of her right hand and slapped it against her left palm. A long while before, the girls in 407 had taught themselves some sign language. This was the sign for "fail." Faith pressed her lips together and sadly shook her head.

The bell rang at the end of the period and all the girls gathered their books and notebooks.

"Dumb stupid fancy essay test," Casey said as she, Faith, and Dana met going out of the room. "Dumb spot test."

"Oh, come on, Case. Happens all the time," Faith said.

"I know. That's one of the troubles with Canby Hall."

Faith and Dana exchanged glances behind Casey's back. Their friend, Casey — small, freckled, tomboyish, full of fun and smart, too — was really a "poor little rich girl." Her parents were internationally known art dealers who traveled around the world so much and were so busy that, as Casey used to say, "They send me photos every once in a while so I'll be able to recognize them when they pick me up at the train station." Casey had been the school's most imaginative rule-breaker and caused a lot of problems for herself. Then, last year, helped and abetted by friends, school, and her own good efforts, she started to get it all together. Dana and Faith knew that she could still be moody and difficult sometimes — and those were the times she was most likely to get into trouble.

"And let's try to guess what MacPoison will

do to me tomorrow," Casey said.

"She's not so bad. She tries to be fair, you know that," Dana said.

"Take it easy, Case, please," Faith said.

"Who needs any of it!" Casey exclaimed, breaking away from them and storming down the hall.

"Uh-oh," Dana said, looking after her.

"Maybe she'll watch her soap opera after classes. That usually cools her down," Faith said. "I'm worried. I wish I could hang around with her this afternoon, but I've got to be at the *Clarion*. We're laying out that picture story about traditions and symbols, and nobody knows it but me. I'll catch up with her tonight."

"I hope MacPherson's not too tough tomorrow," Dana said.

"So do I," Faith said.

They both watched Casey disappear down the stairs, then went together into social studies.

After classes that day, a swarm of soap opera regulars sprawled in front of the big television set in the student lounge watching their favorite soap. Casey was among them, slumped on a couch, frowning, legs stretched out, ankles crossed, arms clenched tightly across her chest.

"Don't believe a word he says, Agatha," she sneered at the characters on the screen.

"That actress is Mercedes Johnson," Pamela

said in her superior way. "She's a friend of my mother's. She's had four facelifts."

"Nobody has four facelifts," Casey grumbled.

"Mercedes did. My mother said so and it's true," Pamela said indignantly.

"Is it true about your friend, Grant Andrews?" the character in the soap opera said.

"How many's your mother had?" Casey asked.

"She couldn't possibly need one. She's too beautiful," Pamela answered with a sneer on her own beautiful face. "How many has *your* mother had?"

"None yet, thank you."

"Cut it out, you two. We want to hear this," said Joan Barr, who was sitting on the floor.

Casey growled and muttered, but then quieted down and watched the big screen. In her bad moods, Casey hated, on principle, to comply with any request, even a reasonable one like Joan's, but she didn't want the dumb dueling match with Pamela anyway. She wanted to bury herself in the troubles of the people on the screen. It kept her mind away from her own.

When the soap ended and girls began to stream away from the set, Casey remained scrunched up and frowning. She wished there were another soap to watch but *As the World Spins* was the last for the day. Casey was upset and scared. She had drawn a blank on that test — if they only had had some warning, if it hadn't been so unexpected. When she was trying to write it, she had felt as though every cell in her brain was going off in a different direction. She hadn't been able to connect one thought to another. What a school! When they started giving you tests without telling you you were going to get them, and then flunked you just like that. . . . What was going to happen to her tomorrow? What would MacPherson do next?

Pamela sauntered over to the couch where Casey was frowning even harder, scrunched up even tighter, and stood directly in front of her. Pamela's beautiful face — blue eyes wide, golden hair shining, pouty mouth glowing with a perfect-colored lipstick — had its usual nasty expression.

"That's what you get when you go to a crummy school," she said.

"Thanks a million," Casey answered scornfully.

Pamela smiled. She had an undying grudge against the 407 girls and anything and anybody that mattered to them, and here was Casey, their good friend, ripe for her to win over. People at a low point, like Casey, were Pamela's natural prey.

"Ellie and Mary Beth and I are going into Greenleaf to get some decent food," she said. "Do you want to come with us?"

Casey unclasped her arms and shook them out. She had been clutching them so hard they ached. Then she pulled herself up from the couch and looked at Pamela. She hesitated. Casey really hated Pamela. Casey was an expert on getting herself into trouble, but Pamela's idea of fun was to sneak around and make trouble for somebody else. Still, Casey didn't see any of her great pals anywhere. Obviously none of them wanted her company this afternoon. Going into Greenleaf with Loathsome Pamela might be the perfect way to celebrate flunking English.

Casey looked at Pamela, shrugged, and picked up her coat. "Sure. Why not? Anything to get away from here," she said.

About a half hour later, Faith came to the student lounge looking for Casey. Laying out the picture story had gone faster than she expected and she thought Casey might like some supportive company.

"Anybody here seen Casey Flint?" she asked.

"I did. She left a long time ago, with Pamela Young and a couple of other kids," Joan Barr said, barely looking up from the television screen. Joan was the school TV freak.

"With Pamela?" Faith asked sharply. "Where'd they go?"

Joan, intent on the John Wayne movie, shrugged. Faith suddenly felt uncertain. She was Casey's friend, not her keeper. But she wanted to be sure the friend was okay.

What would Casey be doing hanging out with Pamela? Not much, Faith decided. Casey disliked Pamela as much as the rest of them did. They probably weren't doing anything, just going back to the dorm. If so, Case might have poked her head into Room 407 for TLC. Faith decided to go back to the dorm herself and find out.

At the edge of the park, the shortcut to the dorm, she saw Shelley walking quickly from the opposite direction, from the path that went by the old Canby farm and carriage house.

"Hey, Shel," she called. "Going back to Baker?"

Shelley looked up, flustered. She seemed to pause for a moment before she answered, as though she didn't quite recognize Faith. "Hi. Yes. Sure," she finally said.

Faith shifted her books and waited for Shelley to catch up with her. Shelley seemed distracted. "Hey, are you all right?" Faith asked.

"Sure," Shelley answered.

They started to walk across the park toward Baker House.

"I'm hunting Casey," Faith said. "When last seen, she was with Pamela and I have this awful feeling that she shouldn't be — not today of all days."

"Why not today especially?" asked Shelley.

"We got our exams back in English today and Casey flunked. Then, when Ms. Mac tried to talk to her about it, there was a little run-in."

"Oh, no," Shelley said. "Casey must really be upset. I can't imagine anyone going tough with Ms. Mac." Ms. MacPherson was the drama coach and Shelley's favorite faculty member.

"Case was really thrown when she failed that test. I mean bad," Faith said.

"Not to worry," Shelley said. "She's probably in her room right this minute. We'll find her and cheer her up and that'll cheer you up, too, won't it?" Shelley linked her arm through Faith's and they hurried to the dorm.

CHAPTER EIGHT

In the Greenleaf supermarket, Pamela didn't just choose any shopping cart. She pulled one, then another, then another out of the row of carts neatly nested into each other along the wall near the exit.

"They're all junk," she said, pulling out a fourth, a fifth, trying to find one that didn't rattle or that rolled smoothly enough to please her. When she finally made a choice and walked off with it, she left all the other carts as an obstacle course for the grocery-laden shoppers going out to their cars. A security guard, muttering about spoiled brats, went over to put the carts back in place.

Pamela halted at the start of one aisle.

"This is how we shop in here," she explained to Casey, who was slouching next to her.

"Yeah, tell me," Casey said. "I've never been in a supermarket before."

Pamela made a sound somewhere between a snort and a chuckle and Casey stepped back in mock alarm.

"You laugh!" she said.

Pamela smiled at that and Casey could not help herself; she smiled back. It was a little smile, and wry, but even so, it was Casey's first sign of brightness since the morning.

"Okay," she said, "explain your system."

"It's just that we stay together, we start over there —" Pamela pointed to the shelves of bottled drinks "— and go up and down all the aisles before we go to the freezers."

"No problem. Off we go!" exclaimed Casey. She grabbed the handle of the cart and rolled it so hard it almost hit a display stand.

"Be careful, Casey," Pamela said, pushing Casey's hand away.

"Don't push me," Casey said.

"Come on, then." For Pamela, that was conciliatory.

The girls went to the first aisle with Pamela directing, Casey feeling a little more perky, and Ellie and Mary Beth both developing supermarket glaze — that is, the expression of people who are so absorbed studying shelves, finding what they're looking for, deciding which of what to buy, and checking prices, that they don't notice anything else.

"I wish I had the nerve to get a six-pack of beer," Casey said as she slung a six-pack of diet soda into the basket.

"Why don't you?" Pamela said. "I dare you."

"Come off it," Casey answered.

"I heard you were the only fun person at Canby Hall until they tamed you down, Casey." Pamela smiled sweetly, watching to see if her barb had hit home.

"Right," Casey said, giving their cart a hard push, startling a town woman with a small baby who was heaping Coke bottles into hers. "Let me explain something to you, Pamela," she continued, steering around the woman. "Given your limited perceptions, you may not understand this, but I'll try to make it clear. If I really wanted beer, I'd get it."

"Okay," Pamela said. "I didn't say a word."

Casey gave her a quick, quizzical look. Was it possible that Pamela was human?

Cheryl Stern, a Baker House girl, appeared at the other end of the aisle, stocking up on jars of peanuts. When she saw Casey with Pamela and Pamela's pals, her mouth literally dropped open.

"Hiya," she stammered when she recovered. Casey grinned and cocked a finger in greeting.

"See ya, Cheryl," Casey said.

Still surprised, Cheryl looked after them as they passed her and turned into the next aisle.

"You know, you and I are practically related," Pamela said to Casey as the girls paused to decide about cookies.

"No, we're not," Casey said. Ellie selected a bag of chocolate chip cookies from a shelf and dropped it into the cart. Mary Beth stood in front of the opposite shelf with her finger at her mouth, trying to make a decision.

Pamela pressed on. "When my mother was in London last year making a movie, she met your mother and father there and bought a very expensive painting from them. That makes us — well, you know what I mean."

"You mean we both have rich, famous parents," Casey said.

Pamela was only slightly flustered by Casey's directness. She put her beautiful chin up in the air. "Yes," she answered, "except of course my mother is much more famous than yours."

"I don't think that makes us so lucky. Do you? Really?"

"I certainly do," Pamela said, giving the cart a shove. "My mother gives me anything I —"

"Hey, look out!"

But it was too late. The edge of the basket got caught on a corner of a shelf of baking goods and jostled it hard, making two giant-sized bags of sugar at the very top begin to teeter. Pamela jerked the cart back but it stayed stuck and before anybody knew what was happening, one of the bags fell over, ripped and spilled sugar like a waterfall down to the floor. The other bag crashed directly to the floor, bursting and spewing sugar all over the aisle.

Some of the nearest shoppers, startled, turned around. One of them frowned at the girls. A man in a faded lumberjacket very carefully guided his shopping cart around the sugar.

"It almost hit me," Ellie gasped, pointing to the bag with her toe.

As another bag of sugar teetered on the shelf, the girls ran over to save it, scattering the sugar on the floor up and down the aisle.

Pamela, giggling, pointed. "Look!" A young woman whose cart was piled high with a week's worth of groceries had turned so abruptly she knocked over some items on the top of her cart. As she frantically reached to catch her groceries, she knocked into a ketchup display, spattering ketchup over the sugar. The woman was furious and bent down to gather up her purchases. Casey tried to help her but slipped and fell into the mess of sticky sugar. She wasn't cut by the glass — her coat protected her — but the ketchupy sugar was all over her. Mary Beth started to laugh so hard she doubled over, holding her hand over her mouth. And when Ellie went over to help Casey up, Casey, also laughing, tossed loose sugar at her.

"I don't know any of you," Pamela said, grabbing the cart and running down the aisle away from them. Casey quickly got up, dripping sugar, and with Ellie and Mary Beth close behind, ran after her.

"Bad spill in aisle three," a voice announced over the PA system.

"They're playing our song," Casey laughed, and they all streaked even faster for the far end of the market, incredulous shoppers staring after them.

"Hey, stop that," one of them shouted to their backs.

"Kids!" another complained to the stranger next to her.

A little girl about four wiggled loose from her mother's hand and, laughing loudly, raced after them, her mother in wild pursuit. A baby started to cry. Tearing around a corner, the little girl's mother knocked over a cardboard display and scattered its boxes of cakes directly in the way of Pam and Ellie, who couldn't avoid stepping on them and squashing them with their boots.

Suddenly the girls discovered they were running into the store's security guard and stock boys, and that the manager of the supermarket was striding toward them, eyes blazing.

The girls stopped running but they couldn't stop laughing. Casey bent over, trying to catch her breath. She crackled; the sugar and ketchup had hardened in spots all over her coat. The little girl who ran after them was snatched up by her exasperated mother. Ellie looked down at her boots, now encrusted with cake, and thought they were excruciatingly funny. Then all the girls saw the supermarket manager standing in front of them, legs apart, fists on his hips.

"What's going on here?" he demanded.

Suddenly they realized that they had gone wild, that they were in real trouble. Ellie stopped laughing and looked frightened. Mary Beth turned as white as the little wool cap she was wearing and Casey went pale, too. Pamela, however, being Pamela, hid her fear behind a show of bravado.

"What do you kids think you're doing?" the manager asked furiously.

"Don't get into an uproar," Pamela said haughtily. "It's no big deal . . . a little sugar spilled, that's all."

"Is that so?" the manager asked. "No big deal?"

Pamela maintained her pose while the other girls looked at her in astonishment. "What happened that's so awful?" Pamela asked.

"You've caused two bags of sugar to break, a display of ketchup to mess up the sugar and six cakes to be ruined. You've disrupted my store and my customers, and you're fresh in addition to all that."

"My mother will pay for the damages. Just send her the bill."

"Well, thank you, young lady. I'm real glad to hear that," the manager said sarcastically.

Pamela smiled her silkiest, nastiest smile. "My mother happens to be Yvonne Young. She'll pay for everything, and give you an autographed picture if you'd like."

"I don't want any picture," he said.

"You're making a big mistake. It's a gorgeous picture. But anyway, she'll pay the paltry sum, whatever it is."

He rocked on his heels for a moment, looking at Pamela.

"Shut up," Casey whispered.

"Money isn't what this is about," he said finally. "Don't you really know that?"

He signaled to the security guard.

"Fred, take these girls to my office and keep them there. Tom," he said to one of the clerks, "cordon off that aisle and the display. I don't want it cleaned up yet." Then he turned to the customers who were looking on and said, "Sorry for the inconvenience, folks," and with that, went over to take a look at the scene of the rampage.

The security guard ushered them into the manager's small, glass-enclosed office where they instantly became the main attraction for shoppers waiting in line at the checkout counters, who looked, pointed, buzzed, shook their heads. The little girl who ran after them waved as she left with her bag-laden mother.

"I wish they'd stop staring at us," Mary Beth whimpered.

The guard self-consciously posted himself outside the tiny enclosure. Soon the manager came into his office. He didn't say a word to the girls, just glanced at them, seated himself at the plain wood chair at his desk and, with his back to them, busily went to work on some papers. The girls huddled together.

"What's going to happen?" Ellie whispered.

"Nothing. He's just trying scare tactics," Pamela whispered back. "Mary Beth, do you have some Kleenex? I must clean off my jacket."

"You've got nerves of iron, I'll give that to you, Pamela," Casey whispered.

"But what will he do?" Mary Beth murmured.

"He's not going to do anything. I told you," Pamela whispered.

They were quiet for awhile.

"Do you think he called the police?" Ellie asked in a low whisper.

"Wash your mouth out," Casey answered. She began to take her ketchup-and-sugar-encrusted coat off, then changed her mind.

A half hour dragged by. The manager never looked back at them.

"Can you get into a good college with a police record?" Mary Beth asked softly.

"I'm not going to wait forever," Pamela said finally. She stamped up to where the man sat and put one hand on her hip, Hollywood-style. "We've had quite enough of this," she said to the manager.

"Oh, you have?" said the manager. "Well, I'll tell you something. I've had enough, too. You've had some time now, waiting here, to think about what you did and to say you're sorry. I've been sitting right here and I haven't heard you say that. Any of you. Now just sit down and wait until I'm ready for you to go. And when you do go," he added, "don't come back for a month. I don't want —"

He was about to go on when he saw something over Pamela's shoulder and abruptly walked by the four girls as if they weren't there, out of the office. He was a big, heavy man and his footsteps made the wood floor shake. The girls watched as he went to the "In" door of the market and greeted the two women who were coming in.

"Allardyce!" Ellie whispered. "It's Miss Allardyce and Alison Cavanaugh." Ellie lived in Addison House but she knew Baker's houseparent. All of them knew the headmistress of Canby Hall.

"I wish it were the police," Casey said out of the corner of her mouth when she saw the expression on the headmistress' face.

As the three adults moved toward the small office, Pamela pranced out to meet them. "Miss Allardyce, my mother will —"

"I'll talk to you later, Pamela. I'll talk to all of you later." Her voice sent shivers down Casey's back.

The girls, even Pamela, didn't dare move or speak as the manager escorted their headmistress and houseparent to inspect the aisle with the ketchup now congealed into the sugar, the shards of broken glass glittering in the debris, and the smashed-up boxes of cake. They stood huddled together, watching, as the group came back toward them.

"If I could talk to you for another moment?" the manager said, and the girls watched him draw their headmistress to one side, out of earshot.

"We're going to be expelled," Ellie whispered in a voice like death.

"No, just sent to jail," Casey said.

"Nothing will happen," Pamela insisted. "Allardyce will give us one of her idiotic speeches. That's all."

"I was going to call the police," the manager was saying quietly to Miss Allardyce, "but since it's Canby Hall and, okay, kids get out of control sometimes, I called you instead. All I want is full payment for damages . . . and . . ." he turned and spoke loudly enough for the girls to hear, ". . . I don't want those girls in this store for a month."

"I understand your position exactly and I apologize for my girls," Miss Allardyce said, her face tight with anger.

"That's more than your girls have done," the manager said.

Pamela, furious, stomped up to the manager. "So we can't come into your silly little market for a month. Who cares? There are a lot of other stores in town."

The manager looked Pamela up and down thoughtfully. "You've got a lesson to learn, kiddie. And somehow I'm going to see that you learn it."

CHAPTER
NINE

Even Pamela didn't say anything as the four girls marched out of the supermarket, Allardyce ahead of them, Alison not quite but almost behind them. In silence they walked the few paces to Allardyce's car while people who had been in or around the store when all the excitement was going on stood stolidly and stared at them or buzzed in small groups. They were like prisoners being led into the paddy wagon, Casey thought.

Casey glanced at the others. As usual, Pamela was behaving like a glamor girl, swinging her curves in their custom-tailored jeans, pulling the collar of her mauve down jacket up around her face as though it were sable. Ellie, head down, looked thoroughly abashed, and Mary Beth once again was as white as her cap.

Casey felt her ears getting hot and she stared straight ahead. The three other girls were exchanging the little signals of old friends but she felt alone, left out. She tried to swagger the few steps to the car but wasn't extremely successful. Miss Allardyce was directly in front of her and even the back of her neck was formidable.

"It will be a tight squeeze," the headmistress said briskly when they got to her car. "Mary Beth, you're the smallest. You sit up front between Miss Cavanaugh and me."

As the others scrambled into the back seat, they made faces to each other and groaned silently for Mary Ellen's sake. Casey lifted her eyes in thanksgiving that it wasn't her up there, squeezed between the two women. Alison was all right, but imagine being hip to hip with Allardyce!

Once the ride began, Ellie tried to explain.

"A lot of it was an accident, Miss Allardyce," she said. "The bag fell down and. . . ."

"If they had stacked it properly, nothing would have happened at all," Pamela interrupted. "In fact, we probably ought to sue them for negligence. Ouch!"

Casey had jammed an elbow into her ribs. They were in bad enough trouble without Pamela pushing.

"We won't discuss this matter at all until we get back to Canby Hall," Miss Allardyce announced.

Casey and Ellie exchange apprehensive glances. They knew it was bad now and was going to get worse. Alison looked back and made a small quieting motion with her hand. Casey sat back and crossed her arms and Ellie looked stricken, but Pamela just shrugged.

In the ensuing silence, the girls in the back heard Mary Beth sniffle and saw Alison hand her something, probably a Kleenex. Mary Beth had used up her supply, wringing them into shreds during their terrible wait in the supermarket. Pamela stared out the window. "The nerve of that man, running like a baby to Allardyce," she was muttering.

Ellie and Casey exchanged glances.

"What'll Allardyce do?" Ellie whispered.

"No clue," Casey whispered back.

"Could she expel us?"

"She could do anything," Casey answered softly. She wished Alison would turn around and maybe smile at them.

Ellie pushed her honey-colored hair back from her eyes. "This is terrible. My mother will kill me if she finds out. Oh, boy."

Casey didn't know what her parents would do. If Casey got expelled or even suspended, they might actually make her go to the school in Europe they had talked about before she'd pulled herself together and acknowledged that she loved Canby Hall.

To keep herself from her thoughts, Casey studied Miss Allardyce's car. She'd never seen it from the inside before, just its shining black exterior parked in Miss Allardyce's driveway, or running through the campus. Kept in very good condition, Casey noticed. Not even scratched on the leather armrest. *Same car she's had since I came,* Casey thought.

In the front seat, Alison was looking as straight ahead as Allardyce. In a row, facing forward, Casey looked at Alison's thick brown hair, Mary Beth's little white cap, Allardyce in a big fur beret. Alison's arm was across the top of the front seat. Casey wondered whether her heavy glove, near Mary Beth's shoulder, was giving Mary Beth a little comforting touch, a pat.

The palms of Casey's hands were getting awfully damp. She breathed deeply. She was positive Allardyce was taking a new, unfamiliar, ten-times-as-long route back to school.

Miss Allardyce stopped the car in front of Baker House and the girls tumbled out. "Go inside, clean up, and come directly to my house," she ordered. Alison stayed behind for a moment, listening, answering, nodding, agreeing.

Faith opened the door of the dorm from inside before any of the girls could reach a hand out. "At last!" she exclaimed.

Dana had been just coming into the dorm when Alison rushed out toward Allardyce's house. "She looked so upset I asked her if anything was wrong and she didn't exactly answer so I knew something *was* wrong," she told her roommates. That, combined with Faith's concern about Casey had brought Dana, Faith, and Shelley into the dorm lounge to wait for them to come back.

Alison glanced at her watch. "You might miss dinner. I'll ask the dining hall to prepare some sandwiches. They'll be ready when you get there. Now I think you'd better get up to your rooms, clean up quickly, and get downstairs and to Miss Allardyce's as fast as you can. I'll be in my apartment in case anyone needs me." Alison was Alison, but she wasn't smiling.

"What happened?" Shelley demanded as they were going up the stairs.

"Not a thing," said Pamela. "They're making such a stupid mountain out of a molehill. They don't have to worry. My mother's going to pay for everything."

"In other words, we started a riot in the supermarket and Allardyce brought us home," Casey said, half bold, half frightened.

"And wants to see us at her house right away," Mary Beth whimpered, going into her own room where her roommate welcomed her and closed the door behind her.

"Oh, *Case*!" Shelley exclaimed.

"Exactly," said Casey. "Well, thanks for the reception committee."

Casey stopped by 407 on her way out. In

clean jeans and a bright red sweatshirt, she looked scrubbed, freckled, hoydenish — and rebellious.

"Here's the lamb ready for slaughter."

Dana shuddered. "Don't joke," she said.

Shelley rushed up to hug her. "Break a leg, Casey," she said. "That's 'good luck' in theater talk."

"Remember, we love you," Faith said. "Take it easy, Case."

Pamela, with Mary Beth behind her, appeared at the door dressed like a Hollywood princess—soft beige wool pants, a slightly darker beige sweater, and a strand of slightly darker stones that glittered against the sweater. Her eyes were shadowed with a little too much mauve and green, but they, too, glittered, as though she were ready for battle.

"We're ready, Casey. Are you?" she said.

Casey looked at Faith almost wistfully, then grinned. "Sure I am. Do your worst, Patrice baby. I'm ready for you. Farewell, Room 407. Farewell, Baker House. Farewell, Canby Hall, I hope *not*." With that, Casey linked her arm through Pamela's. "Let's go."

"Case, remember, whatever she says, say 'yes,'" Dana called out as the three girls disappeared down the steps.

"I won't even listen, how about that?" Casey called back. The roommates looked at each other in dismay.

*   *   *

In the presence of Patrice Allardyce, it was hard to maintain too swaggering a manner, especially when you knew you were there to be punished.

"As you know," the headmistress finished, "Mr. Ewer will not let you into his supermarket for a month. I have not yet decided whether I will extend that period to the end of the term. Nor have I decided in what other way you will try to make amends. For the present, however, you are confined to the campus for three weeks, you are not to leave the grounds at any time, including the weekends, and all special privileges are revoked. You may go."

"I'm really getting to hate this school," Casey growled at Faith later, walking back to Baker House from the dining hall. "Allardyce is cruddy. Canby Hall girls this, Canby Hall girls that. You'd think this dump was the best place in the world. According to her, if you're really lucky, when you die, you go to Canby Hall instead of heaven." Casey kicked at a stone in the path.

"I know you're angry and scared, Case. And it's tough that we'll have to shop for you at the supermarket. But, hey, being campussed for three weeks isn't as bad as it might have been. I think Allardyce was easy on you."

Casey's bravado collapsed. "I know she was. I thought we'd be suspended, that's what I really thought. I could hear my parents on the phone from Paris. 'But she *can't* be suspended. The house isn't open.' " The girls crossed the park in front of the dorm, past the wishing well. "You should have heard her, Faith. Spitting fire, but icy."

"Well," Faith said, sighing, "I guess it teaches us all over again that we have to stay away from Pamela. How did you get mixed up with her, anyway?"

"Oh, Pamela's not so bad," Casey mumbled.

"Casey, come back to earth!" Faith exclaimed, startled. She felt worried all over again. Casey was getting tangled in her old unhappy feelings and if she decided to latch onto Pamela permanently, terrible things could happen. Pamela was a destructive model for anyone, especially Casey. Allardyce had been fair, Faith thought. This was no joke.

"Awful cold, isn't it?" Casey said, shivering and hugging herself tighter into her down jacket.

"It's getting warmer. Spring's coming," Faith said softly. "It'll be okay, Case, I promise you. Just hang in."

"I still have to see MacPoison tomorrow," Casey said, shuddering.

Faith put her arm around her friend. Sometimes she felt that she was as much of a social worker as her mother down in D.C.

CHAPTER TEN

Dana was out jogging and, hating herself, Shelley was making for the pay telephone in the old Canby carriage house. She knew Randy had tried to call her but it was hard for him; after all, she and Dana lived practically in each other's pockets. If she and Randy were going to be sneaky and underhanded — which is exactly what they were being — then she was the one who had to make these moves.

It was the hour on Sunday when everything was either finished or hadn't begun yet, and nobody, absolutely nobody, was near the carriage house, yet Shelley approached cautiously, almost tiptoeing. She felt that if she simply strode blithely up to the phone, Dana, at the farthest end of the campus, would know exactly what she was doing!

Since their accidental day in Waterville, Shelley and Randy had had one afternoon to-

gether, a few hours after classes when they
had met by arrangement at the far end of
Greenleaf and gone driving through rural
Massachusetts, talking, looking, stopping once
and then again on empty side roads to be together quietly, to kiss, while Shelley protested
what she was doing.

"It's me," she whispered into the phone
when Randy answered it.

"I've been waiting," he said, a smile in his
voice. "Wouldn't let anybody near the phone
for a half hour."

"I couldn't get here sooner. Oh, Randy,
what am I doing?"

"Calling me, Shelley. It's okay."

"No, it's not, but I guess I can't help myself," Shelley said. She hadn't been able to
look directly at Dana all day, all week.

"I don't feel too easy about it, either,"
Randy said. "I'm involved, too."

"That doesn't make me feel much better,"
Shelley answered, so softly he hardly heard
her, so softly she could tell herself she hadn't
even said it.

They made plans to meet at the same place
in Greenleaf they had met before, in an hour,
and Shelley hung up and tiptoed away from
the carriage house. Suddenly she had a
thought: Pamela wouldn't dream of tiptoeing
if she were doing something sneaky. She'd
just prance along, calmly and confidently.

Shelley immediately shifted into her usual stride. Then she stopped in her tracks. Was she really admiring the way Pamela would act? Was she trying to imitate Pamela?

By the time she got to Greenleaf, walked past the supermarket with averted eye, and ambled through the particular residential street that led to the meeting place, Shelley felt entangled in a terrible mix of emotions. She had to face herself as somebody not too different from Pamela, somebody not very decent anymore. Yet she couldn't control the surge of gladness she felt when she saw Randy's truck parked by the corner, and Randy standing next to it looking for her, waiting for her, his cowboy hat down over his cool, gray eyes, his quirky smile greeting her. As she found herself hurrying to him, her conscience stabbed her so hard it was almost a physical pain.

In the truck, she studied Randy's lean, handsome face. He had taken his hat off and his face was now framed by soft, golden hair. She reached out and touched it. Was it for this she was deceiving one of her best friends, her roommate? Under her hand, his hair felt like straight and shining silk. Distracted for a moment, she put her hand on her own hair for comparison. It was crisp and curly, different altogether. She put both her hands in her lap. She didn't like not liking herself.

The truck rattled along its way, out into countryside. "Where are we going?" she asked in a small voice.

Randy smiled down at her. He found Shelley very endearing, even though the fact made him feel uncomfortable and disloyal to Dana. He was not a particularly introspective boy, but he instinctively knew that Shelley filled a space in him that Dana — who intrigued him more, who interested him more, whom he loved more — somehow left empty.

"I thought out to my place and saddle up a couple of horses. How does that sound to you?"

Shelley sat upright, her self-flagellation ended.

"Terrific," she exclaimed. "I haven't been riding since this summer at home." She sat back with a sigh of pleasure. "I love that idea, Randy," she said.

They drove along the fences, up to the house and beyond it, directly to the stables. Shelley helped him saddle both the horse he chose for her to ride and his own favorite hacker. Then he helped her mount and watched intently, squinting a little in the sharp sunlight, as she settled herself in the saddle, took the reins, bent to adjust her stirrups, and talked softly to the horse. Then he mounted and led the way out.

"There are some trails beyond the pasture," he said over his shoulder.

They spent a couple of hours on the

trails; walking, trotting, cantering, galloping through the woods where the last of autumn's leaves crackled as they passed, and the late afternoon light turned the shadows of trees into waving spikes of black. When it was over, they came walking the horses back to the stables, flushed, cleareyed, tired, and happy.

"This was as perfect as a day at home," she told him. "You wouldn't think I'd want a day to be like at home, would you, but, well, I don't know. . . ." She shrugged, one shoulder only, not wanting to go on.

"I think I know what you mean," said Randy. "Isn't it like the way things were when you were a kid blending into the way things are now, when you're grown up, almost grown up? Something like that?"

"Maybe," Shelley said. Dana had talked about, complained about, Randy's empathy and, Shelley thought, here it was.

They dismounted; Randy unsaddled the horses, put them back into their stalls, made sure the stable boy was there to tend them, and came back to Shelley, rubbing his hands together.

"If I didn't like them so much, I'd say I could eat a horse. How about you?"

"Starving. As always," Shelley sighed with a smile.

"Come on into the house. I'll scramble up some eggs."

"No, I'd rather not," Shelley said.

"You're kidding," Randy answered.

"No, I'm not. Can't we go to the village and get something there? Pizza? Hamburgers? Something? Scrambled eggs, if that's what you feel like. Please, Randy." Her voice was serious.

"What's the matter, Shelley?"

"I . . . It's a little hard to explain," she began. "I've been seeing you and. . . ." She took his hand. ". . . I love it, I loved riding with you, I lo — *enjoy* just being with you. . . ."

"But?"

"I'm Dana's friend, you know." Shelley's tone was bitter.

"I know," Randy said gently.

"Anyway, she's told us about the wonderful times she's had with you and your family in the house, the brunches in your big kitchen, all of that . . . and I simply don't want to go in there. Inside the house, well, belongs to Dana."

Randy pushed his cowboy hat back on his head and peered down at her.

"I don't exactly understand, but you're the boss. Whatever you say."

Shelley squeezed his arm.

"Hop in," he said, opening the door of the truck. "We'll go into Waterville, to our diner near the library. How about that?"

"Terrific."

Shelley studied him as he took one last look around to make sure everything was in order, and then got in next to her and started driving. *The truth is,* she thought, *you are terrifically handsome, and graceful in the way you move and I could watch you forever and there are other things, too, but the main thing is you're wonderfully comfortable to be with, Randy Crowell, like Paul, and I don't want to stop seeing you and I don't know what I'm going to do about this. I really don't.*

Randy started to sing "Red River Valley," completely wiping serious thoughts out of her mind. They were singing "Greensleaves" at the top of their lungs, not very well, when Randy slowed up in front of the diner. Suddenly Shelley stopped singing and grabbed his arm.

"Keep driving, keep driving," she muttered hard. "Keep driving."

Randy accelerated immediately. Shelley had gone dead white.

"Pamela Young was on the street. She saw us," she said in anguish.

Randy was confused. "Not possible. You said she's campussed."

"Trust Pamela to break the rules. I don't know how she got here, but that was Pamela."

"Ah, she didn't see us," Randy said.

"I think she did," Shelley said. "She certainly recognized your truck, and she had to know that the girl in it wasn't Dana."

"I think we better ride toward Greenleaf," he said. "On side roads," he added. "But we'll stop and get something to eat first."

Shelley burst into tears. Randy, startled, grabbed a box of Kleenex out of the glove compartment and pushed it into her hands.

"Ah, Shel," he said.

"I don't know what to do," she wailed. "I shouldn't be here, I shouldn't. . . ."

"Shel, don't," Randy pleaded. "I'm sure you're wrong about Pamela. She's back at Canby Hall. She couldn't be in Waterville. Please don't cry. Ah, Shelley."

"The te-te-terrible thing is, I don't want to stop seeing you, Randy," she sobbed. "I had a wonderful d-d-day with you and . . . and. . . ." She bent over, her head in her lap, shaking in her misery. Suddenly she stopped shaking, and stopped crying, too. Instead, she started to sniff. She put her nose against her thigh, against one inner knee and then the other, down her legs.

"Oh, Randy," she groaned. "I smell of horse. If I get near my roommates, either of them, before I get these jeans in the washing machine, they'll know! Oh, what am I going to do?" She started to cry again, this time even more bitterly than before. Randy pulled over to the side of the road and gathered her up into his arms, rocked her, kissed the tears away. Then he rolled the window down.

"We'll freeze," Shelley exclaimed.

"It's the only thing I can think of to air you out unless you want to walk back to school."

Shelley caught on and laughed. Randy was absolutely right. She was just seeing shadows.

It couldn't possibly have been Pamela back there — and it certainly would be better to get rid of the horse smell by driving with the windows open than by walking. She pulled her down jacket up around her waist, feeling foolish.

They stopped, finally, for hamburgers. Looking at Randy across the table from her, Shelley decided it was the kind of day that becomes a special memory.

CHAPTER ELEVEN

If only she could be sure!

Shelley sat at her desk, staring out of the window, not seeing the thin, unceasing rain. She was wondering. It was her newest occupation. Ever since Sunday, she had been in a monumental daze. Even the supermarket excitement had only temporarily brought her out of it. All she could think of was pulling up to the coffee shop in Waterville and seeing Pamela, or *not* seeing Pamela, or *was* it Pamela? She could hardly concentrate on anything but her uncertainty. Only a moment ago Faith had said something interesting about something but Shelley couldn't remember what, and now, her book and notebook open in front of her, she tried and couldn't even think about her preparation for French, her nemesis.

Every day since Sunday — and every night — she had tossed and turned, cold shivers running down her back at the thought that Pamela might have seen her and Randy together. Randy kept telling her it wasn't possible. Pamela was campussed at Canby Hall. Even Pamela wouldn't risk being expelled by leaving the campus when she wasn't allowed to. And certainly Pamela never hinted anything when they saw each other. The person outside the diner was someone else, someone Shelley just imagined looked like Pamela. Randy was sure and he was probably right but Shelley was feeling that you couldn't be sure of anything, especially at three or four in the morning, with a guilty conscience keeping you wide awake.

"Wow, that was a big one," Faith said.

Shelley was startled. "What?" she said.

"That sigh. Poor lamb, you sounded as though the weight of the world was upon you."

Shelley shook her head. "No," she said.

"Well, that's good," and Faith on her bed, sneakers off, feet up the wall, returned to reading her favorite magazine, *General Photographer*.

The door opened with a bang and Dana came in, boots wet, yellow slicker dripping, hair glistening with rain, and arms filled with a big parcel post package.

"Hey, look, something from home."

Faith peered over the top of her magazine.

"It's bigger than a breadbox. . . ."

"Yep," said Dana, lowering herself cross-legged on the floor. "Heavier, too," she said.

Faith swung herself down and off the bed and tested the weight of the box. "Certainly is," she agreed.

Shelley, although interested, stayed at her desk. It wasn't always easy to come close to her friend whom she was deceiving.

"Rattle it, Dana. See what kind of noise it makes," she said from where she sat.

Dana shook the box. "It rattles," she said. She put the box on the floor, shrugged herself out of her coat, and pushed her hair back from where it fell damply against her cheek. "I don't think it's food. I don't know what it is," she said.

"I have this terrific idea," Faith said.

Dana laughed. "You're right. I'll open it!"

She tore off the brown paper and picked up a little white envelope on top of the red-striped gift wrapping.

" 'For when schoolwork is not monopolizing your time. Lots of love, Dad and Eve,' " the card inside read. "From my Dad. And Eve," she said. "Isn't that nice?"

"What *is* it? Hurry!" Shelley said. In her entire life, Shelley had never been able to wait to unwrap birthday presents.

"Just a second, just one second," Dana said, busily unwrapping the pretty paper. Finally it was all off and the present revealed: a new and shining game of Monopoly.

"Terrific!" Dana exclaimed. She opened the box and took out the board, the cards, the paper money, and the instruction sheet. Shelley couldn't resist. Soon all three girls were on their knees, heads together.

"I'm ready to play this minute," Faith said. She looked up at the Mickey Mouse clock on their wall. "I think we have time before dinner."

Pushing the box to one side, they opened the board on the floor, counted out the money, and were ready to start when Faith sat back on her heels.

"Listen, let's ask Casey in. She likes this game and even though she's pretending tough, I think she feels rotten."

Shelley scrambled to her feet. "Good idea. I'll get her." Enormous waves of guilt swept over her when something like this happened, when the three of them were gathered together, cozy, sharing. She'd feel more at ease if Casey, or almost anyone else, was with them. "I'll get her," Shelley said. "Don't start till we get back."

When she saw that Casey's room was empty, she went next door, to Cheryl and Gloria's.

"Seen Casey?" she asked.

"Uh-uh. She doesn't come in here much anymore," Cheryl said, toweling her just-washed hair. "Try Pamela's room."

Since the day of the supermarket, the day of the English marks, the day they were campussed, Casey had been hanging out with Pamela more than anybody in 407 — almost anybody in the whole dorm — could believe. But going down the hall to Pamela's room would be a last resort.

I'll try the lounge, Shelley thought. Maybe she's getting some stuff at the food machines in the Ping-Pong room.

But as she went downstairs, it was Pamela, not Casey, she saw coming toward her from the Ping-Pong room carrying a handful of peanut bars from the machines.

Shelley assumed her most carefully casual manner.

"I'm looking for Casey," she said. "Have you by any chance seen her?"

"Of course," Pamela said. "She's back there actually thinking about playing Ping-Pong. Grace challenged her." She smiled indulgently.

Suddenly, Shelley wanted very much to talk to Pamela.

Get Casey, an inner voice warned her.

Stay and talk, another one said, not to ask Pamela anything directly, not to say anything significant, just to chat. Just to find out subtly if she's been keeping to the campus. *All you have to do is act as though you think she's so clever she's probably worked out some way to get around being campussed. It'll be all right.*

Don't do it, the first inner voice said.

But the suspense had become intolerable.

Be nonchalant and uninterested, the second voice said. *You know how.*

Pamela was at the bottom of the stairs, coming up straight toward Shelley. It was now or never.

Don't, the first inner voice cried.

"Well, Pamela," Shelley said, laughing lightly. "How's it going with being campussed?"

"Oh, that." Pamela raised one exquisite eyebrow. "It's too stupid for words. The only thing is, off-campus around here is even more stupid than on. Now, if it were New York outside, things would be different."

"Yes, I guess Waterville isn't anything like New York," Shelley said.

"Waterville? What about Waterville?"

"Oh, nothing. I just happened to be out there last Sunday and I thought I saw you. Isn't that dumb?"

"Why would I be in Waterville, that dinky town?" Pamela asked.

"I don't know. I just thought I saw you there. Outside the coffee shop near the library. Randy and I —" She went scarlet. "*Tom* and I were there for lunch and I thought. . . ."

Pamela's eyes widened but she gave no other sign that she had noticed the correction. She laid a pale, soft hand on Shelley's arm and smiled her nastiest, meanest smile.

"No, Shelley, I wouldn't dream of going to Waterville," she said. "I'm campussed, don't forget. But I'm so happy that you go there on your dates."

Shelley flushed again. "Well, sometimes I do," she managed to say. She found that her heart had jumped up to her throat. How could she get away? Ah, Casey, of course.

"I can't believe Casey's playing Ping-Pong. Are you sure? That I've got to see."

With what she hoped was a languid, confident manner, Shelley freed herself from Pamela's touch, ambled down the stairs, and turned toward the Ping-Pong room in the back. When she was out of sight of Pamela, she stopped and leaned against a wall. She had to catch her breath and she wanted to bite her tongue off!

Pamela, watching her flee, laughed out loud. And Shelley Hyde thought she was an actress! That was about the worst acting performance Pamela had ever seen. She knew Shelley's slip of the tongue wasn't a slip at all. Shelley certainly hadn't been with Tom on Sunday. Tom had been at Canby Hall looking for her. Pamela had answered the door when he came to Baker House. "I was just passing," he had said in his rather cute way. Pamela hadn't bothered to tell Shelley.

So Shelley was sneaking to Waterville with Dana's Randy. Pamela started to run upstairs, eager to share this gorgeous piece of gossip. Then she slowed down. She decided to keep it to herself for a while.

CHAPTER TWELVE

Faith wanted to return the sweater she had bought.

"The sleeves made me look like I was sprouting wings," she said to Dana as they went through the wrought iron gates, and turned left for Greenleaf.

"I saw," Dana agreed.

"Funny how something can look great when you're in the store and yuck when you get it home."

"Yeah."

"They had a pale yellow coat sweater I almost bought. I hope they still have it," Faith said, shifting the box from Fancy Dress from one hip to the other.

"Let's try Teen Togs, too. Cheryl said they had cute heavy sweat shirts."

"Sure," Faith said. "And I need film."

"We're running out of diet soda," Dana remembered.

"Right."

They walked companionably along the road to town.

"And I'll get a care package for Casey," Faith said. "She needs it. Boy, how I'd hate to be campussed. I mean, I love dear old Canby but not to be able to even step off the grounds. . . ."

"Casey went bonkers. I thought those days were over," Dana said.

"So did I," Faith said. "The thing that worries me is the way she's taking it." There was a sharp, cold wind blowing and Faith dug into the pockets of her down jacket for her mittens. "It's like the old Casey," Faith went on. "I have a terrible feeling she may even start pulling some of her old tricks. Correction! Think up new ones, and get herself into worse trouble."

Despite herself, Dana smiled. "Casey sure was inventive. Do you remember when she called people and used Allardyce's name to order things like flowers, and pizzas, and a hearse from the pet cemetery and — what was that gigantic thing they needed two men to unload?"

"A whirlpool bath from the rental shop," Faith added dismally.

"That's it, and Casey would sit at her window with binoculars and watch them being delivered to Allardyce's house."

"Funny," Faith said, "but not funny."

"I know it's not," Dana said somberly.

"She hasn't thought about doing wild stuff like that for the longest time." Faith shook her head. "Until now."

"You know, Faith, Pamela is *evil*. Even if the thing at the supermarket started as an accident, when Pamela's involved, things always turn terrible."

A motorcycle came zooming toward them, went past them, circled back, and pulled up next to them.

"Ladies!" Tom swept his helmet off and bowed as gallantly as he could from the seat. "Can I give you a lift to Canby Hall?"

"Thanks, Tom. We happen to be going in the other direction," Faith said, laughing.

"I knew there was something different about you," Tom said. "Well, then, if you won't ride with me. . . ." He revved up the motorcycle. ". . . I'll just go on my way. Shelley's expecting me."

"Is she?" Dana said. "I thought she was going to Waterville this afternoon — to take back that book."

"I think she has a date with me," Tom said. "It's been too long since I've seen sweet Shelley," and he zoomed away.

"Is Shelley cooling off Tom?" Dana asked. "I didn't know that."

"I don't think so," Faith said. "She hasn't mentioned anything to me."

"Or me. But I don't think Shelley and I

have had a gabfest in weeks. I've been so busy. When the concert's over, I'll have time again." She slapped her arms against her sides. "Hey, is it me or is it getting colder?"

"It's colder again," Faith said. "Dana, for my sake, please give up that club next year."

As loyal roommates, Faith and Shelley always went to Dana's Choral Club concerts but neither of them, no matter how hard they tried, genuinely enjoyed the medieval music.

"You sound like Randy," Dana said, laughing.

Faith sighed. It had been a losing battle for three terms.

"Well, I'll bring my camera," Faith said, and they discussed such things and others until they found themselves in front of Tutti-Frutti, the ice cream place of Greenleaf.

"Now or later?" Dana asked.

"Now. Nothing like some refreshing ice cream to warm you up when you're almost frozen," Faith said with a grin. "Me for a banana split." A town mother and her little boy, licking ice cream cones, came out as they went in.

There were only a few people, all from town, in the ice cream store — three women with shopping bags relaxing over sundaes at one of the little tables and a man waiting while Charlie, the boy behind the counter, filled a quart container for him to take out. As always, before they sat at a table, the girls greeted Charlie and went to the display case to study the flavors. Dana peered intently at what looked like specs of chocolate, nuts, and candied fruit in a swirl of cherry-vanilla.

"Is this new, Charlie? What is it?" Dana asked after the boy finished with his customer.

"I can't tell," Charlie said in a muffled voice.

"Who could?" Faith said, looking where Dana was looking and laughing.

"I mean, I can't tell you," the boy repeated. "I can't serve you. You can't come in here."

Dana looked up. "What'd you say?"

"Tutti-Frutti's closed to Canby Hall for two weeks starting yesterday," Charlie said softly, quickly, as though that's what he had been told to say and was obeying. He seemed uneasy and avoided looking directly at either girl.

"Oh, come on. Charlie. Don't make jokes," Faith said. "I'd like just a plain banana split, please — vanilla, chocolate, strawberry, chocolate sauce, lots of whipped cream."

"Can't," he said again. "You have to leave."

"We just got here," Dana protested.

"I can't help it. You can't stay."

Faith held her hands up. "Wait a minute. Charlie, are you seriously saying you won't serve my friend and me? That you don't want us in here?"

"It's not my idea. That's what they told me to tell any girl from Canby Hall who came in."

"I don't believe this," Dana exclaimed.

"Can we buy cones and take them out?"

"No," Charlie muttered.

The women at the table came up to the counter to pay their check and glanced at the girls curiously. Faith and Dana stood casually, quietly.

"Why don't they want us?" Faith asked sharply when the women left. "Do you know, Charlie?"

"No," the boy said, shaking his head. "I don't know any more, except, no kidding, I've gotta ask you to leave."

"Okay! Okay! We're going," Faith said.

With all the dignity they could muster, the girls fastened their coats and left.

"See you in two weeks," Charlie called after them with forced good cheer.

"Did you just hear what I heard?" Dana exclaimed indignantly as they stood out on the sidewalk. "What on earth happened?"

"I haven't a clue," Faith answered.

"I think it's outrageous," Dana declared angrily. "They don't have any right to do that."

"They seem to be doing it," Faith said. "Simmer down, Dana. Let's go exchange my sweater."

"But I . . . I. . . ."

"We can't do anything about it now. Let's get the sweater thing over with and poke around some. Maybe somebody else knows what happened," Faith said.

Dana's anger collapsed and they started walking slowly away.

"It's funny, isn't it," Dana said after a while, looking back over her shoulder at the Tutti-Frutti. "I feel real peculiar. I never had anything like this happen before. It's crazy. It doesn't make sense."

They turned onto the main street and began walking toward The Fancy Dress.

"If we get desperate, I guess Randy or Johnny or Tom can go to Tutti-Frutti for us," Dana said after a while. "Hey! We can get ice cream pops at the supermarket when we get the soda."

"Good thinking."

Faith shifted the box with the sweater from one arm to the other. As they reached the store, they saw Mrs. Harrison, a short, plump, and very blonde saleswoman, putting a scarf back in the window. Faith tapped on the window and smiled when Mrs. Harrison looked up.

"Ho," Faith said as the saleswoman left the window and met them at the door. "I came to return this sweater." She offered the woman the box, but Mrs. Harrison shook her head. "I only bought it last week and never wore it, just tried it on once. . . ."

"I'm sorry, my dear. You'll have to come back in two weeks."

"What do you mean?" Dana asked quietly.

"I guess you girls haven't been in town very

long today or you would know already. I do believe no Canby Hall girl will be welcome in Greenleaf stores for two weeks."

"What is this about, Mrs. Harrison? What's happened?" Faith asked.

"My dear, some Canby Hall girls misbehaved very badly over at the supermarket last week."

"Right. We know that. They're being punished. They're campussed. They can't leave the grounds of the school for three weeks. But what's that got to do with us?" Dana asked. "We didn't do anything."

"But you also are from Canby Hall, aren't you, dear?"

Faith paused. "What about my sweater, Mrs. Harrison?" she asked coolly.

Mrs. Harrison shook her head. "Bring it back in two weeks."

The girls exchanged eye signals.

"How many of the other stores are in on this?" Faith asked, although she was sure she knew the answer.

"All of them," Mrs. Harrison said with a little smile.

"I see," Faith said as courteously as she could. "Thank you."

"Well, I don't see," Dana said when they were out of sight of The Fancy Dress. "It makes me mad. This isn't one bit fair."

"Just pray the camera shop's okay," Faith said. "I have to have film."

At the camera shop, Faith's particular buddy, with whom she had spent, she estimated, five thousand and four hours talking photography, shook his head when she came in. "Two weeks," he said.

They didn't even try the supermarket. When they walked by the entrance, which they had to do, a security guard looked them up and down and gestured for them to stay out.

"I think we better go back to school," Faith said. "This is badsville."

"I'm . . . I'm a little scared," Dana said, trying to laugh. "Listen, let's take a taxi."

"Good thinking," Faith said. Both girls wanted to get back to their school, their home, just as swiftly as they could.

"Nobody's going to believe this," Faith said as the taxi left Greenleaf.

CHAPTER THIRTEEN

Nobody did believe them, especially not Shelley.

"But not all of them can be. Jim Whiting at my jewelry store, he owns the store, we're friends. He wouldn't make me leave if I went in there."

"Do we have to hit you over the head, Shelley?" Dana said. "The stores in Greenleaf are closed to Canby Hall."

"But Jim likes us," Shelley protested. "He comes to spring play every year. Sometimes I get containers of coffee for him and when he's not busy, we sit around in his store, talking about things."

"Go see for yourself," Dana said with a laugh.

"I will," Shelley answered back. Suddenly she wondered if she had spoken too sharply; were her guilt feelings making her angry at Dana? She hurried to soften her tone. "I'll just go and check out a couple of stores you guys missed. Corroboration, isn't that the word?"

Ginny Weissberg burst into the room. "Hey, guess what."

"We know. We've been in Greenleaf, too."

"But I absolutely have to get my mother a birthday present, and mail it this weekend," Ginny said indignantly.

Casey slunk in and collapsed like a rag on the floor near Faith's bed.

"Casey, do you know about this?" Faith asked.

"The stores? Yeah. I heard about it. Being campussed, I haven't had personal experience, but word gets around."

"What really happened at the supermarket?" Shelley asked.

"Well, Pamela bad-mouthed the manager. He said we couldn't come into his place again for another month and she kept talking. . . ."

"I can imagine," Dana said.

". . . so it looks as though he got the other storekeepers to gang up on us."

"Poor us," Shelley wailed.

"'Poor us' nothing," Faith exclaimed. "Boiling in oil is too good for Pamela Young. I bet when news of this gets to our Miss Allardyce, the campussing you four got is going to be like nothing. If the stores in Greenleaf don't want Canby Hall girls around, that means, children, that the school has been disgraced and we're all going to be in trouble."

Shelley riffled through her handbag for a coin. "I just have to see this for myself. Right now," she said, and dashed off to the phone booths on the first floor. Happily, there was a phone free.

"Tom? Oh, I'm so glad you're there. I need a favor. Can you come out with your motor-cycle and take me to Greenleaf? I have to check something and be back in an hour."

Tom didn't answer for a moment.

"Will I really get to see you for a whole hour, Shelley?" he finally said, with obvious sarcasm in his voice. "From now on I'll just stand by the phone and wait for your call. That way you won't have to trouble yourself trying to remember our dates."

"Oh, Tom, I am so terribly sorry. We *did* have a date this afternoon, didn't we? I got so involved with Ms. Mac discussing what the spring play will be this year that I completely lost track of —"

"That makes two in a row, Shel," Tom interrupted.

"Two?" she said, puzzled. All of a sudden her face went white. Sunday! The Sunday she had spent horseback riding with Randy. She and Tom had made plans to see a movie that same afternoon. How could she have for-gotten? And twice in a row!

"Tom, I'm not sure what to say," she began. "I know it's not much of an excuse but things have been really crazy here. We're trying to keep Casey out of trouble . . . and . . . well . . . I guess I've just been very absentminded lately. I am so sorry. . . ." Her voice trailed off.

"You do want to see me, don't you, Shelley?" Tom said. His voice was quiet and hesitant. He didn't sound his jovial, confident self.

"Oh, Tom, of course I do." She was having trouble keeping her voice steady.

"Well, then, that's all that matters," he said after a pause.

Shelley wondered if Tom could hear her heart pounding. It sounded like a beating drum to her. Could he possibly have seen her and Randy together? she wondered.

"We're both so busy with school and all, even *I* might forget a date — I don't know about *two*, but. . . ." His voice was teasing now; he sounded like familiar Tom again.

Shelley hoped he didn't hear her sigh of relief. "Now, don't you go apologizing. It really is my fault and it's not going to happen again. I promise."

"That's good enough for me. So, what's this about needing a lift to Greenleaf?"

"If you could, Tom, I'd really appreciate it."

"Bundle up, my deario. I'll be right there," he said.

"Thanks a million, Tom. You're too good to me." She made the tone light and Tom cheerfully agreed with her and hung up. But then, still holding the phone, she breathed the words again, softly, changing them slightly: "Tom, you're too good *for* me," she said.

"Tom's coming," said Shelley, coming back into the room. She went to the mirror, tangled her hair with her fingers and retrieved her jacket from the closet.

"Hey, we can outfox 'em a little," Faith said. "Ask him to go into Tutti-Frutti and get us some ice cream."

"Great idea. Tom Terrific," Dana said, smiling at Shelley. "And when Randy comes tomorrow, maybe he'll bring us a pizza."

"We're lucky we've each got a good guy to depend on," Faith said.

A look of anguish swept across Shelley's face, and abruptly she turned to her bureau, pulled out a drawer, and rummaged around in it, mumbling something about finding a scarf. There was a tap on the door. Only then did she turn back into the room.

"Shelley, visitor downstairs."

Dana got up and went to the window. "It's Tom's motorcycle," she said. "He must have flown."

"That's because he's an angel," Faith said.

Shelley sighed, bundled herself into her jacket, and left.

* * *

After Shelley left, Dana said, "I think we ought to tell Alison; maybe she doesn't know."

The girls had been angry, confused, surprised, shocked; but now the shivery feeling they had had in town returned, the one that had sent them back to school in a taxi. It was a little as though solid ground had fallen away and they didn't know where to walk.

"You're right," Faith agreed, untangling herself from the floor.

"Not me, thanks," Casey said with her tough laugh.

"Me, either," said Ginny. "I want to know if anybody else knows anything."

Alison welcomed them in. Her wild mass of wavy, reddish-brown hair was, as usual, a little out of control but, as always, her warm, understanding energy was running full force. She looked from one face to the other.

"Serious?" she asked.

"It's strange and serious," Faith said, while Dana nodded.

"Have a cup of tea? And old-fashioned, bad-for-you cookies?" Alison was inclined toward health food. "My mother sent them to me," she said wryly.

Over tea and cookies, the girls told her about the Tutti-Frutti and the dress store and the camera shop, the complete narrative of their afternoon in town.

"Mrs. Harrison at Fancy Dress said it had to do with that day at the supermarket," Dana said.

"Shelley didn't believe us at all," said Faith. "She's gone to town herself to prove that we were wrong. But she won't be able to."

"That *is* serious," Alison said when they finished. She reached for her phone. "Let me make a couple of calls. Don't leave," she added as both girls started to get up.

Comforted by Alison's taking over, the girls helped themselves to more cookies, sipped their tea and sat quietly and listened as Alison talked with the houseparents at the other dorms.

"Have any of your girls come back from Greenleaf today with a curious story?" they heard her ask Mrs. Druyan at Addison House. She listened intently, looked over at them and nodded. The same thing happened when she spoke to Mrs. Franklin at Charles House.

When she hung up on her last call, she said, "Yes, other girls are reporting this. You can go back to your rooms now. It's almost Study Hours and I have one more call to make." She breathed deeply. "I've been elected to tell Miss Allardyce," she said in a conspiratorial voice.

"We have to do something," Shelley said, storming into 407 one minute before Study Hours.

"She believes us now," Dana said to Faith.

"It was humiliating," Shelley said, throwing her coat into the closet. "They all asked me to leave, just like that. Just like you said," she added, a little abashed. "We have to do something about it!"

"It's been done," Faith said. "You missed it. We went to Alison, and Alison's on her way to Allardyce. The lioness has started to roar."

CHAPTER FOURTEEN

No Canby Hall girls saw her — and if they had, they probably wouldn't have believed their eyes — but when their headmistress heard Alison's report, she slapped her hand against her desk so hard she had to pace up and down her study, phone cradled between her shoulder and ear, alternately waving the hand in the air and blowing on it to ease the pain.

"We will interrupt Study Hours this evening," she told Alison. "I want to see the four girls who were at the supermarket here immediately. Three of them are in your dorm. Will you see to them, please. I will call Charles House myself." She looked up at the portrait of Horace Canby that hung over the fireplace, and looked away from his gaze. The wealthy industrialist had established Canby Hall as a school for girls on his property as a tribute to his only child and heir, Julia, who died of fever when she was twelve. That was one hundred years ago and in all the time since there never had been any real conflict between the school and town. This one had to be halted as quickly as possible.

"I'll go quietly," Casey said, throwing up her hands in mock terror when Alison came to her room. But Alison didn't smile.

"I wish you weren't involved in this, Casey," she said. "You haven't been in any kind of trouble the whole year, and now this."

"That's the way it goes sometimes, Alison," Casey said.

"It doesn't have to," Alison said, responding gently to the false bravado. "You don't have to be the bad girl to let us know you're here and that you're important. You're important without that, Casey."

Casey set her mouth tight for a moment.

"Okay," she said. "But you did come to get me, didn't you?"

"Yes. Miss Allardyce wants to see you, Pamela, and Mary Beth right away. Ellie, too, of course."

Shelley was coming out of the bathroom when the three girls were going down the stairs.

"Hey, what's with you?" she called to them.

"We're paying a call across campus," Casey tossed over her shoulder.

Shelley ran after them. "Allardyce?" she asked in a whisper.

"Nobody else," Casey said.

"Because of the stores?"

"Who knows? Probably."

"Oh, Casey," Shelley groaned. "Be careful. You, too, Mary Beth."

"I'm also going, Shelley," Pamela said insinuatingly.

Ever since the encounter on the stairs, Shelley felt extremely uncomfortable in Pamela's presence and tried to avoid her as much as possible without either the discomfort or the avoidance showing. She forced a smile.

"Oh, sure, Pamela, good luck," she said and then huddled over her friend.

"Listen, Casey, come into 407 the minute you get back," she said, still whispering. Seeing Alison waiting at the bottom of the steps, she stood back and watched them go the rest of the way down.

"What do you think Allardyce wants?" Mary Beth asked pitifully.

"It's the store thing," Ellie said to Pamela as they walked together to the headmistress' house, worried and disconsolate.

"Not at all," said Pamela.

"Want to bet?" asked Casey.

Mary Beth had started to cry.

"Oh, come on, MB," Casey said, "Act like a lioness."

"I don't feel like one," she said. "I feel terrible."

"We all do," said Ellie.

"Well, just don't forget we have to stick together," Pamela said, "although I can't imagine why everybody's carrying on like this. My mother will pay. . . ."

"Didn't you hear what the man at the supermarket said?" Ellie interrupted, irritated. "It isn't a matter of money."

The girls paused when they reached the house.

"I seem to have lost my breath," Casey said, with a choked laugh.

"That's called panic," Ellie said. "I feel the same way."

"What will she do?" Mary Beth asked.

Pamela pranced up to the door, smoothed her eyebrows, and rang the bell.

"Well," she said. "Let's find out."

The old housekeeper, Anna, opened the door, said, "Yes, you're expected," and pointed them toward the headmistress' study.

Standing in the middle of the room, Patrice Allardyce silently watched each girl come in — Pamela with her head defiantly high, Casey swaggering, Ellie at a sort of slink, and Mary Beth as though her knees had completely melted. The silence dragged on as she examined them, one after another. After a while, Ellie and Mary Beth began to send nervous messages to each other and Pamela had to look away, but Casey looked back at Miss Allardyce, determined not to drop her eyes; it would mean defeat. Finally, Miss Allardyce spoke.

"I'm not going to ask you to sit down. This will be brief. As I'm sure you know, the stores of Greenleaf have decided they do not want the patronage of Canby Hall girls for two weeks. Although you are campussed yourself and this does not, therefore, directly affect you, I am sure you can understand how the other girls feel not being able to go into our local stores. Much more distressing, however, is the fact that this extreme action has come about because of your behavior. That this school should be responsible for such a high degree of bad feeling among Greenleaf's merchants is a reflection on Canby Hall that I will not tolerate."

Casey's mouth went so dry she was afraid she was going to cough. She felt they would all blow up if anybody else made a sound.

The headmistress took a deep breath. "I have made inquiries. It appears that your extraordinary rudeness to the manager of the supermarket has led him to organize this boycott against Canby Hall. Would any of you care to comment?"

The girls waited for Pamela to say something but she maintained a look of guileless innocence. The pause lengthened until finally Ellie cleared her throat.

"I guess one of us *was* sort of rude," she managed to say.

"I see," Miss Allardyce said, waiting.

When it was clear that Pamela was not going to speak, she continued.

"Your rudeness, and only that, triggered this situation," she said. "Such being the case, you four must be the ones to try to end it as quickly as possible. To start, I'm sure each of you will want to write a letter of heartfelt apology to the manager of the supermarket. If you wish, tomorrow morning before classes you can give your letters to my secretary and she will see that they are delivered. The manager's name is Philip Ewer. Spell it correctly, please. E-W-E-R. That will be all for now."

"Pamela, you're too much," Ellie said as soon as they had crossed the wide lawn of the headmistress' house. "How could you stand there and not admit you were the one?"

"That man was very rude to *us*, don't forget," Pamela said self-righteously.

"He had pretty good reason to be," Casey said.

"I don't know what you mean," Pamela said.

Casey sent a pleading glance skyward as they walked into the birch grove, the shortcut back to the dorms. "'That'll be all for *now*,'" she said dispiritedly. "I wonder what she's got lined up for tomorrow."

"Do you suppose our letters to Mr. Ewer will make a difference at the other stores?" Mary Beth asked.

"What letters?" Pamela said. "I have no intention of writing one. After all, my mother's going to pay for everything."

"Of course you have to write an apology," Ellie said. "For heaven's sakes, aren't you sorry? We were disgusting in that supermarket — and look what happened. The whole town turned against us."

"No, I'm not all that sorry. It was sort of fun, wasn't it?"

Casey leaned back with an incredulous look of admiration.

"Let Allardyce jump around in circles if she wants. I don't allow myself to collapse every time somebody says, 'Naughty, Naughty.' That's nothing but a sign of weakness."

"Do whatever you want to but I'm going to write a letter," Ellie said seriously.

"Me, too," Mary Beth said in a small voice.

"How about you, Casey?" Pamela asked. "You on my side?"

Casey felt trapped, the way she always used to feel. "Well, I'm not going to write any letter tonight. I have to finish an extra essay for old MacPoison. One evening of writing is enough for me."

"Did you hear that, Ellie?" Pamela said sharply. "You're wrong to do what Allardyce says. We all have to stick together."

"No, *you're* wrong, Pamela," Ellie retorted. "And you know it, too, Casey," she said. "We've made it tough for the whole school — no ice cream, no pizza, no market. I heard even the movie theaters won't let us in."

"They won't be able to hold out for two weeks," Pamela said in her superior manner. "Maybe they think they're hurting us but they're really hurting themselves. The stores in that little town need Canby Hall. If it weren't for us, they wouldn't be able to stay in business."

"I'm not so sure of that," Casey said. "But I'm willing to find out."

"Good for you, Case," Pamela said. "And anyway," she added, as though it were the real clincher to the argument, "what difference does it make to us? We're campussed. We can't go to any of the stores anyway. Even if they can hold out for two weeks, by the time our campussing is over, they'll be open. How about that!"

"Pamela, you're incredible," said Ellie. "I don't think I realized until this minute that you aren't even human."

"Very funny," Pamela said scornfully.

"I agree with you, Ellie," Mary Beth said in her little voice.

Pamela started to put her arm around Casey's shoulder but Casey shrugged it off.

"Oh, let's get back to the dorm," Casey said, walking quickly away from all of them.

CHAPTER FIFTEEN

Shelley had taken her textbook and tape recorder and gone to the little room. "That way I can recite my French without disturbing you," she told her roommates.

The little room down the hall was, literally, a tiny room that Baker House reserved for girls who wanted to study by themselves, without distraction. More and more frequently, Shelley used it as a way of coping with her problem: feeling not only uncomfortable but angry when she was with Dana.

But after a while, as she sat leafing through her book, she knew she had to go back to 407. The news had spread through Baker House quicker than fire, first that the stores were closed against Canby Hall and then that Allardyce had called Pamela, Casey, and Mary Beth out of Study Hours because of it. Every room on the second floor vibrated with waiting for them to get back and Shelley couldn't bear not sharing the suspense. When Shelley opened the door, Dana leaned back in her chair and folded her arms.

"I give up, too," Dana said. "I have three chapters of social studies to finish reading tonight and I can't get it done," she said.

"How long have they been gone?" Faith asked.

"Almost an hour," Shelley said. "I feel like a pregnant father."

"Like a what?" Dana asked.

"Translated, that means this waiting is hard. I'm with you, Shel," Faith said.

"What's the worst thing that can happen?" Shelley wondered.

"Suspension, I would guess," Dana answered. "A few days, a week, something like that. It's very bad, being sent home."

"What's the least that can happen?"

The noise level in the hall suddenly rose.

"They're back," Faith exclaimed, and all three girls hurried out. Casey, Pamela, and Mary Beth were coming down the hall. To everybody's surprise, the first of them to speak was Mary Beth.

"I apologize to you all," she said. Her voice was little, as always, but rang with determination and dignity. "It's our fault that the stores are closed. Miss Allardyce says the first step is, we each have to write a letter apologizing to Mr. Ewer at the supermarket but I thought we owed you an apology, too. I'm going to write my letter now." With that, she cut through the surprised girls and went directly to her room.

"Why, Mary Beth's a real lioness," Shelley said.

"She's chicken. So's Ellie," Pamela said angrily, pushing toward her room. "Casey and I aren't writing any abject apologies," she added smugly. "We're waiting for the stores in Greenleaf to apologize to us, aren't we, Casey?"

"I'm not abject for anybody," Casey said.

"Of course not," Pamela said.

Faith ignored Pamela. "Casey, is that really *all* you have to do? Send the man an apology?"

Everybody else in the hall gathered around. This concerned all of them.

"For now, I guess," Casey answered.

"A written apology doesn't sound so awful, considering you smashed up his store," Shelley said.

"And were rude afterwards," Dana added. "Didn't you insult that store manager, Pamela?"

"I'd hardly call it that. He was much more insulting to us," Pamela said.

"Oh, Pamela," Faith said in exasperation.

Alison appeared, taking in the scene. "Break it up, girls," she said.

Girls clustered around her but Alison was not inclined toward conversation.

"It's still Study Hours," she said. "Now, get going. Pamela and Casey, I'm sure you want to go to your rooms." With that, she turned, and went toward the stairs.

As the hall emptied, comments went drifting through the air: "Better do it, Case," "If it'll open the stores. . . ." "You got off easy," "You *have* to, Casey," "You both better change your minds." There was a chorus agreeing to that last one.

Faith saw Casey hesitate.

"So go, Case," she said. "Get your paper, get your pen, and write the thing."

"Cool it, Faith. I'm not about to write anything but an essay for MacPoison."

"You're kidding."

"Nope."

"Casey!" Faith exclaimed in despair.

"Faith!" Casey exclaimed back, imitating her, grinning a tomboy grin.

"How much time do you have?" Faith finally asked. "Did Allardyce give you a deadline?"

"Oh, she said something cute about delivering the letter tomorrow morning."

"Then what, Casey?"

Casey shrugged. "Haven't a clue," she said. "Pretty exciting, isn't it?"

"Coming, Casey?" Pamela called from down the hall.

"Yep." Casey grinned impishly at Faith and left.

"I could strangle her," Faith said when she was back in 407, attempting to finish English homework.

"Which one?" Dana asked.

"Oh, Pamela's hopeless. I mean Casey. She knows better. She's on her way to really serious trouble and is pulling that I-don't-care number."

"Do you think she's being led astray?" Shelley asked.

Dana laughed. "Shelley, I love your vocabulary."

"Please don't laugh at me, Dana."

"But that's such a wonderful, ancient expression. Even my grandmother doesn't say 'led astray,'" Dana said.

"I think that's exactly what's happening to Casey," Shelley said sharply. "I think Pamela *is* leading her astray. Without Pamela, I bet Casey would be writing her letter of apology this minute."

"Maybe she is anyway," Faith said, trying to calm them down.

"Let's hope so," said Dana.

The next day, Faith and Grace Barish, the school paper's best reporter-photographer team, were sitting around the *Clarion* office. Faith was slumped into a hard wood chair, her feet up on the battered table that was used to lay out the school paper, and Grace perched at the edge of the table twiddling a pencil.

"Well, what do you think?" Grace asked. "Do we do a *Clarion* feature on the Greenleaf stores?"

"I guess so," Faith said. "It's certainly a news story. I could get pictures from the outside of the stores looking in, but will you be able to interview anybody? I bet not."

Grace shrugged. "I hear the boycott may last a long time. Your pal and Pamela won't write the apology letters."

"I know," Faith said glumly. "What did Ellie do?"

"She went straight to her room and wrote the letter. You know Ellie. She's not going to hold out long."

Pamela passed the open door and Grace called out to her. Pamela came into the room, smiling her usual sticky smile.

"Pamela, are you going to apologize or not?" Grace asked.

"Of course not," Pamela said indignantly. "I'm the one waiting for an apology."

"You really are unbelievable," Faith said with contempt.

"Oh, you're so superior, aren't you?" Pamela said. "You and your roommates, you're all such perfect beings. Doesn't it get a little heavy sometimes wearing that big halo?"

"What's this got to do with my roommates? We're talking about you — and why you're not writing that letter," Faith said.

"I'm not writing it because I have guts. That's more than I can say for some people. Although . . ." she paused, put her head to one side, rested one of her fingers on her beautiful cheek, and looked at Faith slyly. "Although I guess you might say one of your roommates likes to take chances."

"What's that supposed to mean? Oh, Pamela, I can't be bothered with you," Faith said.

"No, nothing bothers you. Nothing bothers any of the paragons in 407. You wouldn't even be bothered if you knew that your roommate's been having wild, romantic dates with Randy Crowell in Waterville, would you?"

"Wow! Hot news," Grace said sarcastically.

Faith shook her head.

"What's wrong with you, Pamela?" Faith asked. "So what, Waterville? Dana and Randy go together. They can go anywhere they want to."

"Of course. The only thing is, I didn't mean Dana. You have more than one roommate."

"What are you talking about?" Faith demanded.

"Well, if I don't mean Dana, who's your other roommate?" Pamela smiled triumphantly at the uncertain looks Faith and Grace exchanged.

"Oh, cut it out, Pamela," Faith said in disgust.

"Ask her yourself."

With that, she walked out of the room, looking back over her shoulder to wave gaily at the two girls who stood there looking puzzled.

"Do you believe her?" Grace asked.

Faith blew out her breath. "I don't *want* to believe her."

"Ah, I just don't think it's possible," Grace said. "Shelley's . . . Shelley, but that's too dirty a trick. I mean. . . ."

They looked at each other, neither wanting to take her thoughts much further.

"This one's mine, Grace. She's my room-mate," Faith said finally. "Will you give me your word not to say anything until I find out?"

"I promise. . . . You all right, Faith?" Grace asked softly.

"No, I'm not. I'm furious. But I don't know whether it's at Pamela, whom I hate, or at Shelley, whom I love."

CHAPTER SIXTEEN

Two days later, Mary Beth and Ellie had delivered their letters, but the stores were still closed to Canby Hall; Pamela and Casey were still holding out. At the end of the day, a notice was posted on bulletin boards throughout the school and, to make certain nobody missed it, in each dorm the houseparents called a meeting to make an announcement. The meeting in Baker House took place in the downstairs lounge just before Study Hours. The girls settled themselves on the floor, the chairs, the sofas, the arms of the chairs and sofas, and some stood, leaning against the walls.

"In case you haven't seen the notice, Miss Allardyce has called a general assembly in the auditorium of Main Building tomorrow morning," Alison began. "It's called for eight-thirty and...."

There was a mass groan which Alison stopped immediately.

"Look, I feel pretty rotten that girls from my dorm have been responsible for some serious trouble at this school so no complaints from you about the hour, please. Just be on time, every one of you. All right? That's it."

The girls looked at each other out of the corners of their eyes and left the lounge quickly and quietly. They went up to their rooms feeling nervous — Alison's manner had gotten to them — but also very relieved. Patrice Allardyce was a formidable, even mysterious woman, to many of them. In fact, some girls made their priority goal at Canby Hall avoiding one-to-one contact with her at any time. But all the girls knew that in times of trouble the headmistress was fair and *there* and they trusted her to take care of them in situations they couldn't handle, like the one now, in Greenleaf. Talking, whispering that night, they could only guess what might happen to Pamela Young and Casey Flint, but they knew that they themselves would be all right. Miss Allardyce had taken charge and she would see to it.

At eight-twenty-five the next morning, the auditorium was filled with two hundred girls, tense and silent.

"I've got the galloping jitters," Dana whispered.

"Me, too," Faith answered. "Do you see Casey anywhere?"

"I saw her come in but — Oh, there she is, in the back, with Pamela," Dana said.

Faith turned and saw Pamela and Casey over on the side, in the next to last row. Nobody was sitting with them. Pamela was holding herself straight, and smiling, still trying to pull off her blameless act, but Casey was slumped in her seat, looking pale and frightened. Faith tried unsuccessfully to catch Casey's eye.

There was a stir, a rustle, and Faith turned to face front as Miss Allardyce came out onto the stage and crossed over to the podium.

"Eight-thirty," Shelley whispered, consulting her watch.

The headmistress was a handsome woman — tall, fair, her light hair pulled up in a tight French twist, her slim figure sheathed in a dark, thin wool suit — but her frostiness reached out and touched each girl.

"Good morning. I'm sorry to have to call you to this assembly . . ." she began.

"A bad beginning," Dana murmured to Faith.

"I'm sure you are all aware that, for the first time since the founding of this school, an unhappy situation exists between the merchants of Greenleaf and Canby Hall. Canby Hall and the town of Greenleaf have depended on each other, supported each other, and lived as good neighbors with each other since the school was founded more than a hundred years ago. This week that harmony was disrupted, and I am deeply distressed to have to say that responsibility for the disruption lies entirely with us at Canby Hall."

No girl had ever heard Miss Allardyce so icily angry. A stir of apprehension swept over the auditorium.

"The boycott by the merchants of Greenleaf," Miss Allardyce continued, "is a direct response to arrogant misbehavior in one store on the part of four Canby Hall girls."

Faith slumped down in her seat. She didn't want to look back at Casey and Pamela.

"I have consulted with the merchant involved. All he requires to end the boycott is a letter of apology from each of the girls. Two of the girls have written such apologies and the apologies have been accepted."

Mary Beth, three rows in front of the 407 girls, looked both proud and weepy as girls in nearby seats tossed her quick, approving nods. Ellie, off to the side, pushed back her honey-colored hair and looked straight ahead even when her roommate nudged her.

Miss Allardyce had not finished.

"That the boycott is continuing," she said with a stinging voice, "is due entirely to the other two girls, Pamela Young and Casey Flint. They also must write letters of apology and so far have refused to do so."

Four or five girls turned to look back at Pamela and Casey. The others stayed rigid in their seats.

"Their refusal is a shocking reflection on

— and of — Canby Hall and every girl in the school, past, present, and future," Miss Allardyce went on. "Pamela and Casey, like all of you, *are* Canby Hall. Therefore, until they deliver their apologies, Canby Hall itself is campussed. Beginning now, every girl is confined to the school grounds."

Miss Allardyce did not respond to the shocked gasp that rang through the auditorium. Her face grim, she simply left the podium and walked off the stage.

The girls had to go straight to classes and although they managed shocked discussions whenever they could, it was only, finally, in the dining hall, that friends could get together and talk it through.

"I can't believe this," Dana exclaimed. "We're being campussed because Pamela and Casey won't write a letter? That's crazy."

"You heard her," Faith said. "Every Canby Hall girl represents Canby Hall at all times, and right now, Canby Hall owes the town of Greenleaf an apology. Frankly, I think it's overkill, but what can we do?"

"Sit on Casey and Pamela," Dana said.

"Where *is* Casey?" Faith asked, looking around the dining hall.

"She told me she wasn't hungry," Cheryl Stern said, looking at the tray she had just put down at the table. "I must say, I'm not either. I was going to Boston next weekend."

"Oh! My choral concert!" Dana said. "But

that's here at school. They won't cancel that, will they?"

"Who knows? What are we going to do about Pamela? She's the real villain of this thing," Faith said.

"And Casey," Dana said.

"Yes, Casey," Faith agreed mournfully. "Except . . . I have an idea she feels as bad about this as we do."

"She should," Shelley said, calmly digging into her salad. Shelley was not nearly as upset as the others about being campussed. She felt rather an enormous sense of relief. Being campussed meant that the weight of her guilty conscience was lifted away without any effort or pain on her part. Shelley didn't have to worry anymore about seeing Randy because now she couldn't see him.

"I guess I understand Allardyce's logic," Faith said, "but I agree with you anyway, Dana. Campussing us all is crazy."

"It's certainly not fair but I don't mind," Shelley said, intent on picking bits of pickle out of the salad dressing.

The unexpected comment wrenched Faith away from her train of thought and shifted her attention sharply to Shelley. Shelley had just said she didn't mind being unfairly restricted to the campus. *Why not?* Faith wondered.

"Why not?" she asked.

Shelley suddenly got more intent on her salad. Had she given herself away?

"Oh, nothing," she said. But she went pale.
Pamela was right, Faith thought, her heart
sinking.

After a moment, Shelley raised her eyes.
Faith's eyes were boring into her and the expression on Faith's face told Shelley, as if Faith
had said the words out loud, that the secret
was out, that Faith knew about her and
Randy. Shelley didn't dare even glance at
Dana, who was absorbed in commiserating
with the others at the table.

Campussing, Casey, and now this! Faith
didn't know what to do about the problems
mounting one after another on her back.

She suddenly wanted to get away, to be by
herself. "I'm going to the *Clarion* office. See
you back at the room," she said, and abruptly
left the dining hall.

Finding the *Clarion* office empty, Faith
didn't know where to settle her body or her
mind. She restlessly walked into the park, past
the statue of the lioness and her cubs. The
campussing was going to be one gigantic re-
strictive inconvenience. She had tried but
couldn't seem to reach Casey, to make her
come back into the fold. And what was she
going to do about her roommates and their
shared boyfriend? Faith was angry and upset
at her friends, and at herself that she couldn't
think of any workable solutions.

She was still so angry when she returned to
Baker House that she slammed the front door,

the noise immediately producing Alison from inside the lounge.

"Well, Faith," Alison said softly, gently.

"I'm sorry, Alison. I didn't meant to slam it so loudly."

Alison gave Faith one of her looks, a quick, friendly, seemingly offhand glance that told Alison the depth and width of a girl's miseries or happiness with uncanny accuracy.

"Let's talk about it, Faith," she said.

"No, thanks, Alison. I'll just. . . ."

"You'll just come on to my apartment and we'll have a good talk. This has been quite a day, hasn't it?"

"More than you know," Faith found herself saying.

It was hard not to feel easy and relaxed in Alison's stylish, kind of funky, apartment, even if you intended to stay cool. As Alison disappeared into the kitchen — Alison always believed in tea with talk — Faith curled herself into one of the bright scatterings of cushions on the floor and decided she would sip the tea but keep her troubles to herself. Alison had her own problems about Casey and Pamela. Faith didn't want to add to them. But it didn't work that way.

"Well, what, Faith?" Alison said as she poured tea into a heavy, handsome pottery mug. She looked up and smiled at Faith. Faith accepted the tea but didn't answer.

"You know," Alison said softly, "You don't have to handle the whole world by yourself."

"My mother says that sometimes," Faith said. "But I don't do that. It's just that, well. . . ." She stopped herself. "It's nothing," she said.

"It's certainly something that the whole school is campussed and that your friend Casey is, in a large part, responsible for it." Gently but firmly, Alison persisted.

Faith picked up the mug but set it down again.

"That troubles me," Faith admitted. "It does seem that my friends trouble me."

"Tell me, Faith."

Suddenly Faith realized that she wanted to tell Alison, that she needed Alison's help.

"It's just so much," she began, and then it poured out. "I can't get through to Casey. You remember my first year here, when she ran away and called me instead of anybody else? I got through to her then, and ever since she's been great, hasn't she? Really working at putting it all together. Now it's as though I'm some alien creature. She gives me the big grin, the big joke, and I can't get through to her to get her to cut it out, to write the letter, to get away from Pamela, to be Casey again."

Faith stopped abruptly.

"That's part of what's getting me," she said more quietly.

"That's a lot by itself," Alison said softly.

"But it's not all. I've got Shelley, too.

Shelley's been going out with Dana's boyfriend. I know it. Pamela knows it. Dana
doesn't know it. And I don't know what to
do."

"Faith, dear, do nothing," Alison said.

"But I have to," Faith protested.

"No, you don't. That's what I mean by
handling the world by yourself. You must let
Shelley and Dana and Dana's boyfriend work
this thing out themselves. You're a good
friend to both girls, but it's *their* problem and
they have to solve it. If it gets too heavy for
them, maybe Michael can help."

"Maybe he can," Faith said. "I always think
Faith has to solve everything. Maybe I should
start thinking school psychologist."

"Good idea," Alison said. "As for Casey,
she's not your responsibility either, but I wish
there were something you *could* do, that *we*
could do."

CHAPTER
SEVENTEEN

After only a few days strictly confined to the grounds of the school — no quick trips to town, no visits to friends off-campus — everybody's temper was frazzled and extraordinary rumors flourished.

The hottest and angriest was about Pamela and Casey, who had made this happen. Pamela still was insisting she would compromise her integrity if she wrote a letter of abject apology to anyone and a girl in Addison House told Cheryl Stern that she heard that Pamela's mother had sent an enormous check to Pamela and told Pamela not to give in. But Shelley had heard that Pamela's mother did not send a check, that she didn't know anything about it. Somebody else knew for a fact that Pamela's mother wrote an apology to Ewer — except that another girl heard that it was to Allardyce — but Allardyce still insisted that Pamela had to write one herself. Someone said Pamela was going to be expelled.

"Oh, I wish it were true," Dana exploded to her roommates and a group of friends who had gathered in 407 on the fourth evening after campussing began.

"I heard that *Casey* was going to be expelled," Ginny Weissberg said, "that Casey said she wouldn't write an apology even if Pamela did."

"I can't believe that one," Faith said. She was trying to take Alison's advice but it was hard not to wonder and worry about Casey.

"I don't believe it, either. Anyway, I heard the exact opposite," said Cheryl Stern. "Nancy told me Casey wanted to apologize but Pamela got her not to."

"That I do believe," Faith said.

"It's time we knew what was really happening," Dana declared.

"Or made something happen," Ginny said. "Who wants to be stuck here and punished and all that just because Casey Flint wants to show us how tough she is and Pamela Young is . . . Pig Pamela!"

"You're right," Dana said. "I think it *is* up to us to do something about Casey and Pamela."

"Allardyce and Alison seem to be just waiting," Cheryl said.

"Let's call a meeting of the whole dorm and see if we can think of a way to get those letters written," Dana said.

There was instant approval.

"Tonight. After Study Hours. We can meet

here," Dana said. Their triple was the largest room on the floor.

"One of us'll have to go around and let the other kids know," Cheryl said.

Ever since that moment the day of assembly, when Faith had caught her being too casual about the campussing, Shelley had made a point of protesting and complaining as hard as everybody else did. Her fervor was mostly on the outside; she was still feeling relieved to be sequestered for a while, but some of it was real. She was enjoying the excitement.

"I'll go," she said before anyone else could.

At seven-thirty a group of angry and determined girls crowded into 407, standing, sitting almost on top of each other, spilling out into the hallway.

"Is everybody here?" Dana asked.

"Everyone except Casey and Pamela," Ginny said with a giggle.

"Fun-*ny*," Dana said. "Listen, we all want the same thing, right? Okay. Any suggestions about what we should do?"

"I have an idea, Dana," Ellie Bolton, who lived on the fourth floor, called out. "Let's just descend on them, first Casey, then Pamela."

"How, descend?" Dana asked.

"Just all of us here go jam into their rooms and not leave until they write the apologies," the girl said.

"Like we're doing now, only not so

friendly?" Cheryl said, trying to get four
elbows out of her ribs.

"Sure. It should work," Dana said. "Did
everybody hear what Ellie said? Does everybody agree?"

"Well, let's go right now," Ginny said.
"Casey first?"

"Casey first," Dana said. They started down
the hall, a thick mass of angry, united girls
flowing toward the last room on the left,
Casey's room. Just as the girls reached the
door, it was flung open and Casey, grinning,
stood facing them.

"You're all welcome," she called out, and
then she laughed at their confusion.

"Casey, everybody in the dorm feels. . . ."
Dana began to make the little speech she had
been rehearsing to herself.

"I know why you're here," Casey said, in-
terrupting her. "I'm writing the apology."

"We don't think it's fair that we're campussed and the stores are closed just because
you won't — what did you say?"

It took a moment for the girls to absorb
the message.

"Oh, Casey, I'm so glad," Faith exclaimed
finally, throwing her arms around her friend.

"It's about time," said Ginny, her anger
only slowly ebbing away.

"You're right," Casey said.

"Are you really going to apologize?" Shelley
asked.

"I am." Casey grinned her impish grin.

"What can I say? I promise I was going to write that letter before I even heard your thundering footsteps. Thanks very much, all of you, for coming by. Come again soon."

A collective wave of warmth went from the girls to Casey. She was always sparkling and fun; it had been awful having to hate her.

"Well, that was pretty simple," Dana said. "I guess we can all go back to our rooms and let you get to it."

"You want to hang around, Faith?" Casey asked as the girls started drifting away.

"Casey, you amaze me," Faith said slowly as she followed Casey into her room. "Why on earth did you wait so long?"

"Good question. I guess I was practicing being a powerful lioness."

Faith drew a deep breath. "Casey, you were...."

"Don't say it, Faith. I've been saying it all to myself for quite a while. Had a lot of discussions with myself." Casey wiped her eyes with the back of her hand. "I don't believe in crying," she said with a thin laugh. "Boy, to get the whole school campussed for something as dumb as not writing an apology! It's been a long time since I was the school bad girl. I forgot how dumb it was."

"Glad to hear you say that," Faith said.

"But I couldn't stop. The old me really took hold."

"And now?" Faith asked.

"Just lead me to paper and pen. When I

get over the shakes." She held a trembling hand out in front of her. "Look," she said.

Faith reached out and gave her friend a bear hug. When they disentangled, Casey sniffed one time more. "Okay," she said, and went to her closet and rummaged until she found what she was hunting for, an elegant-looking, pale blue box. "My never-before-used engraved stationery," she said. "Gift from my mother." She sat down at her desk, took out a sheet of the heavy, pale blue paper, and reached for her ballpoint.

"Do you suppose Shelley would lend me her purple felt tip?"

"Casey!" Faith exclaimed.

"Just kidding," Casey hastened to reassure her. "I think I better make a first draft," she said. Ballpoint in hand, she opened her notebook to a blank page and started to write.

"I'll leave you with your creative muse."

"Stick around. You can help me with the hard words."

Faith laughed and flopped comfortably on the floor, happy that her friend had come back home.

After a long time, Casey sat back and held aloft a pale blue envelope. "Signed, sealed, and ready to be delivered," she said.

"Happy day," Faith answered, hauling herself up. "I think I'll go to bed now."

"I'm going to see Pamela," Casey said.

"Oh, Casey, would you believe. I actually forgot about her," Faith said.

Casey was still holding the envelope when she went into Pamela's room and Pamela saw it immediately.

"Don't tell me you've apologized to that terrible man," she said.

"I did and you have to," Casey answered.

"Not me. You're chicken, Casey. I'm not," Pamela said.

Casey nodded. "Maybe I am but that's how it is, I tell you true."

Pamela sneered, picked up her hairbrush, and started calmly brushing her glistening blonde hair. Even alone in her room, Pamela looked gorgeous. She was wearing a silky-looking bathrobe and fluffy mules with heels.

"Something else," Casey said. "I feel good about myself again. You write that letter and you will, too."

Pamela shrugged her silk-covered shoulders. "But I don't know what you mean," she said. "I feel good about myself now. I feel just *fine.*"

CHAPTER EIGHTEEN

The mass attack on Casey was so successful that Baker House gathered again late the next night to "descend" on Pamela until she, too, wrote her apology. But Pamela met them at the door with her customary arrogance and told them to go back to their rooms.

"I've stood up to meaner than you," she told them. "You don't seem to understand that if I have to be campussed, I don't care if you are, too. I'm not going to give in to your silly pressures. I'm tough, in case you didn't know."

With that, she got into bed and turned the light out, and the girls "descending" stood around in the dark room and just outside, shifting from one foot to the other, feeling foolish. They had to admit defeat. Soon a few of the girls in the back started to leave. Then others did, until finally all of them left, hearing Pamela's tinkling laugh sounding down the hall after them.

"I'm going to kill her, that's all," Dana said when they got back to 407.

"No, we'll probably have to do something more drastic than that," Shelley said.

"I think you're right," Faith said. "I think it's a school matter now, not just Baker House."

"Got any ideas?" Dana asked.

"I have," Faith answered. "It's a terrible idea, one of the world's cruel ones. But I think it always works."

Shelley shuddered.

"Yes, it's that bad," Faith said. "We could ostracize her. Give her the silent treatment. Nobody speaks to her. You don't even acknowledge her presence. You don't sit with her. If she talks to you, you don't take notice," Faith said.

"Whew, that's really awful," Shelley said.

"I know it is," Faith said.

"I'm for it," Dana said. "Look, hasn't Pamela been really awful, too? Didn't she as much as say the reason she's not writing the letter is because it wouldn't make any difference about her own campussing? Well, I think she deserves to be ostracized."

"I do, too," Shelley said. "But it's really a rough thing to do. To act as though somebody doesn't even exist!"

"The roughest," Faith agreed.

"It means the whole school," Dana said. "Do you think everybody would cooperate?"

"I bet they would," Shelley said. "People are really angry."

"I agree," Faith said.

"Okay. Let's say we want to get everybody in the school to ostracize Pamela. How do we get the thing going?" Dana asked.

Faith had been going over that problem. "I guess first the three of us talk to everybody in this dorm and find out what they think. If they say go ahead, then we talk to kids from the other dorms. If they want to do it, too, then it's all signals go," Faith said. "But it's going to take one hundred percent cooperation."

"I could talk to Nancy. She's in Addison House," Dana said. Nancy Plummer and Dana were good friends.

"And I've got Grace in Charles," Faith said. "But first, let's do Baker house. It's too late tonight. Tomorrow let's the three of us talk it up and see what happens."

The next day, they got to all the girls and reported back to each other before dinner. The reception was terrific. Some Baker House girls said they'd be happy never to talk to Pamela again for the rest of their lives.

That evening in the dining hall, the girls from 407 huddled with Nancy and Grace.

"Do you think the kids in your dorm would do it?" Dana asked.

"They're mad enough to do anything," Grace said.

"We are, too, at Addison," Nancy said. "How do we go about it, though?"

"Well, first talk it up to the girls in your dorms and then . . . I guess we have a meeting to figure out exactly what to do and how," Faith said. "First the general agreement and then the logistics."

They sat around for a moment looking at each other.

"This is big, you know," Grace said, "It'll be hard for everybody, it really will."

"Hardest on Pamela, let's hope."

It took several meetings with heated discussions and quiet figuring out before all the girls in the three dorms were in total agreement and a starting time was set.

"D-Day is tomorrow morning at eight o'clock," Dana said at the final meeting in 407 between Dana, Faith, Shelley, Grace, and Nancy.

"Okay. Now, just let me review," Grace said. "We don't talk to her. If she says anything to us, we act as though we didn't hear her. We don't sit next to her in the dining hall or student lounge or anywhere, and if she sits next to us, we get up and go away."

"In other words, we act as though she's completely invisible at all times and places," Dana said.

"This gives me the willies," Nancy said.

"It's cruel and inhuman," Faith agreed, "but I'm beginning to think Pamela is, too."

"We'll go spread the word at our dorm. D-Day, eight a.m. tomorrow," Grace said, rising. "Good luck to us all."

"Same for me," said Nancy, also getting up. "Good luck to us. May it work and may we not be campussed anymore!"

After the other girls left, Faith, Dana, and Shelley went in and out of the rooms in Baker House telling the nervous, troubled, but determined girls that D-Day was upon them. When they finally got back to 407, they crawled into their beds and lay silently awake in the dark.

"Do you think we'll really pull it off?" Dana asked.

"Maybe," Faith answered in the darkness.

"Who can be sure?" Shelley said after a while.

They could have been sure. It turned out to be easier than a lot of worried girls had thought. They almost hadn't realized how their anger at Pamela had been keeping them away from her anyway.

At first Pamela didn't realize what was happening. In English the first morning, she leaned over and asked to borrow a sheet of notebook paper from the girl next to her. The girl didn't answer.

"Hey, did you hear me? Will you lend me some paper?"

Again no answer. Pamela just shrugged and asked the girl behind her. But that girl, too, didn't look up from her book, didn't notice the request.

Pamela glanced around the room in time to catch several girls looking at her before quickly turning away. She wasn't sure what was going on, but it seemed as though something was.

When she walked across the campus to language lab, her next class, she ambled along as always, but when she tried to join this group or that, they seemed to ebb away.

"Is anybody by any chance trying to give me the silent treatment?" she laughingly asked a couple of Baker House girls on the cafeteria line at the dining hall. They went on choosing their lunches as though she weren't there.

"Janie," she said to one of them. "You don't want to be in on such foolishness. Listen, you know my red suede skirt you like so much? I was looking at it last night and, not that it's not gorgeous, but I decided I don't want it anymore. Come up to my room tonight and I'll give it to you."

Janie almost instinctively began to say, "No, thanks," but the girl next to her gave her a little nudge and instead of answering, Janie blanched and grabbed a container of milk and pushed her tray along.

"Your loss," Pamela said, shrugging.

During afternoon classes, and afterwards,

and in the dorm at those most social hours when the girls hung out in each other's rooms or in the lounge before dinner, and all through dinner, and walking back to the dorm, and when girls got together when the day was ending — at all those times, Pamela was as though invisible to her schoolmates. The next day the same thing happened. Pamela went around campus with her head high, trying to laugh at girls she spoke to who wouldn't speak to her. The third day she still hadn't given in.

"I sure hope we can hold out longer than she does," Dana said desperately to Nancy.

On the fourth day, after classes, Pamela strode into the student lounge and went directly to Casey who, with Faith, was watching television.

"Casey, I want to talk to you," she said.

Casey didn't even turn her head.

"Oh, come on. You're not so interested in a rerun of *Charlie's Angels*."

Still Casey didn't respond. Only a flicker of her eyelids told Pamela that Casey heard her, was aware of Pamela's urgency.

Pamela turned on Faith. "You think you're so smart, don't you? What did you do? Brainwash the whole school? Casey! CASEY! I want to talk to you!"

Furious at the lack of answer, Pamela strode to the TV set and turned it off.

"There," she said. "Now you'll listen to me."

Casey and Faith looked at each other.

"Want a Coke, Faith?" Casey said.

"Yeah," Faith answered.

But Pamela wasn't going to let it happen; she wasn't going to let them walk away from her. By now everyone in the student lounge was aware of what was going on. They edged forward slightly, very slightly, very slowly, from the snack area, from the corner where the exercise cassette was going, from the Monopoly game, from the chairs near the magazine racks, making a loose, wide semicircle around the group at the TV set. But Pamela didn't notice them. Raging, furious, she ran to block Casey and Faith.

"You can't do this to me. Now, stop it." She wheeled and faced the silent semicircle. "All of you, stop it. Oh, I'll make you sorry you're pulling this stunt. You, Casey, you're going to be *really sorry*."

The next day she capitulated.

CHAPTER NINETEEN

Joy reigned through the school. Pamela's letter arrived at Miss Allardyce's house early the next morning and within minutes Miss Allardyce canceled the general campussing, although, of course, the original four were still confined. She arranged with Mr. Ewer, and through him the other merchants, to reopen Greenleaf stores to Canby Hall girls. At noontime, the dining hall was practically empty: every girl who thought she could make it between her last morning and first afternoon class had gone into town for a pizza and/or ice cream lunch.

On the following Saturday afternoon, Dana's Choral Club concert went on as originally scheduled. It was, as always, a trial for her roommates.

The faculty director of music at Canby Hall was rather famous for exploring dusty libraries and finding obscure music nobody had ever heard before, and having his small Choral Club perform it for the school and other interested people. Both roommates tried hard to like the music, but after every concert decided that it sounded more like a hundred squeaky birds than anything else. But they loved their roommate so they went each year, and in appreciation, each year Dana threw a little party for them and their boyfriends and a few others. Soft drinks and things to nibble in the lounge at Baker House, courtesy Alison, and then to Greenleaf for pizza.

"I just put my head someplace else while they're singing. I recite speeches from plays to myself, and sometimes poetry if I can remember it. I know I should listen hard and try to like it but I really can't. I really don't," Shelley babbled to Tom.

They had come directly to Baker House after the concert, while Faith stayed behind to do some pictures of the Chorals for the *Clarion*. Her boyfriend, Johnny, was coming later. Shelley and Tom were waiting for Dana and Faith. For Dana and Faith — and Randy.

Shelley was upset by the chances she and Randy were taking. It had been so easy when they were campussed and she hadn't seen him. She hadn't even called him during those few days, but now the problem was beginning again. They had talked briefly, hurriedly, on the phone that morning.

"I can't come to the concert, too many chores that time of day," he said. She had been momentarily relieved. "But I *am* coming to Dana's party afterwards."

"Could you possibly not come?" she had asked.

"I couldn't do that to Dana," he had said miserably and Shelley had agreed. They had been miserable together on the telephone.

Shelley saw him first, loping up the walk without his cowboy hat for a change, his golden hair gleaming, his long and lanky beauty standing out.

"Look, Tom, there's Randy," she said, warning herself to take it easy. She waved to him gaily, naturally — she thought.

But when Randy joined them, Shelley shifted into high exuberance so quickly that it was unnatural even for her. Tom immediately noticed the change. He looked sharply from Shelley to Randy to Shelley again, but they didn't even seem aware of him. Their eyes were locked. Randy seemed a little uneasy and he was the one who finally broke away from the gaze, but it was too late. Tom had seen them.

"Dana's not here yet, Randy," Shelley said brightly. "Faith's taking pictures of her and the other singers for the school paper."

"Sorry I had to miss the music," Randy said.

Shelley grinned up at him. "Are you really?" Then she turned to Tom.

"Randy hates the polyphonic medieval

music even more than Faith and I do," she said. "Dana told us," she hurried to add.

Randy smiled, embarrassed, deliberately not looking at Shelley. Tom didn't say anything. He just narrowed his eyes and watched them both.

"I think I'll go look at that picture-taking," Randy said, smiling awkwardly. "I'll wait and come back with them."

"That's a good idea," Tom said to Randy's back. He thrust his hands in his pockets and glowered.

"What's going on here, Shel?" he demanded as soon as Randy was out of earshot.

"I don't know what you mean," she said.

"I heard some rumors about you and Randy but I didn't believe them. I do now," he said.

"Tom, I can explain...." Tears began welling in her eyes.

"Spare me, Shelley. Save it for Dana. She probably didn't believe the rumors, either."

"Oh, Tom, please. It's been awful," she wailed.

"Tell me about it . . . some other time." He had a coin in his hand, and flicked it to her. "Call me when you grow up," he said.

The coin clattered on the floor and through her tears, through her real distress, Shelley started to laugh.

"Why, Tom Stevenson," she said, "that's a line from a play."

"Tough," Tom said. "My apologies to

Dana," and with that he was off. Shelley could hear his motorcycle scream.

Desolate, frightened, she hurried into one of the small alcoves in the back of the lounge where nobody would see her and tried to curb the flowing tears.

Randy returned to find her there gulping back last tears. "Dana's ready to start the party. We're going to. . . ." He looked around. "Where's Tom?" he asked.

"He saw us, he knew."

"Oh, no," he said sadly.

"I think Tom and I'll be able to straighten this out. I hope we will. But it has to be over between you and me, Randy," she said.

"Yes, you're right." He took her two hands in his. "I'm attracted to you, Shelley. I probably always will be, but we both know we can't date anymore."

Shelley nodded. "I've hated the cheating part. And I know you have." She looked rueful. "We're such good guys and yet we haven't been fair. We've been hurtful to other people, people we care about."

"That's it," he said.

Shelley smiled weakly. "You've been like home, Randy. Things here are so different from home. . . . It was as though you were the perfect combination of home and here."

"We can be good friends, Shelley," he said.

Unexpectedly, tears filled her eyes again

and started to roll slowly down her cheeks as she stood looking at him.

Randy didn't say anything but he took her gently in his arms and leaned his cheek against hers and, easily, in a friendly way, she put her arms up to him. The comfort of his embrace dried her renewed tears and, with his arms around her loosely, her arms loosely around him, all the distressful feelings that had so burdened her from the beginning at Waterville fell away.

They were in the back alcove where she had retreated. She heard people at the other end of the room, but dismissed them as just Baker girls coming in or going out.

Good friends, she thought, with a comfortable feeling as she stood there for a moment listening to the beat of Randy's heart. Suddenly he tore away. She looked up at him but he wasn't looking at her at all. He was looking over her shoulder.

Shelley turned and there, not two feet away from them, stood Dana, a look of total disbelief on her face, and Faith, shocked and furious.

Shelley would never be certain exactly what happened immediately after that moment. She knew that she had called out, that Dana had turned and run and she had run after her, jostling and startling a lounge full of girls. Where Randy went and what Faith did, she never knew. The first she remembered clearly was being on her bed in 407, head buried in the pillow, in tears, and hearing Dana's voice.

"You are the sneakiest so-called friend in the world," Dana was saying.

"I *know*," Shelley answered, sobbing.

"Oh, turn around and look at me," Dana said. "Have you been dating Randy? Have you *really* been going out with my boyfriend?"

Shelley struggled up, raising tear-filled eyes. "Dana, we both felt terrible. But, listen, we're not going to see each other again."

"Am I supposed to be grateful for that?"

"We were saying good-bye when you . . . I mean. . . ."

"You mean when I saw you and the boy I *thought* was my boyfriend locked in each other's arms?" Dana said furiously.

"Yes!" Shelley wailed.

There was a knock on the door.

"Faith, you have a visitor," a voice said.

Faith had been quietly slumped in the farthest corner.

Johnny, she realized. "Tell him I'll be down in a minute," she called.

"Did you know about this?" Dana wheeled to face Faith.

"I suspected," Faith said in a low voice.

"Why didn't you tell me?" Dana demanded.

"I couldn't, Dana," Faith said.

Dana paused.

"Johnny's here for my party, isn't he?" she said.

"I guess he is," Faith said.

"Tell him it's postponed, tell him I'm very sorry, tell him I'll give him a raincheck, tell him . . . anything."

"Oh, Dana, I've ruined your party," Shelley cried, a fresh cascade of tears flowing.

"My party! How about my life? I trusted you. I don't understand, Shelley. I just simply don't understand. Not you, not Randy. I don't understand how this could happen." She strode to the closet, tearing off her concert clothes as she went and grabbing and getting into her jeans and her jogging shoes.

Again there was a knock on the door.

"I'm coming," Faith called with annoyance.

"Two great pals, I must say," Dana said. "I need to get away from both of you."

She ran out of the room, and Shelley turned again to her pillow, sobbing.

CHAPTER TWENTY

She couldn't believe it, that was all. She couldn't understand how it could be. Of all the world's sins among friends, stealing your best friend's boyfriend was one of the worst, and Shelley had done that.

Dana was running, not jogging, on the path across the park and through the maple grove, quiet and away, the path she took when she needed to be alone with her thoughts.

She brushed away tears. *Don't be like Shelley,* she told herself, and cried some more. How could Shelley do this? What started it? Almost more than the fact that Shelley and Randy went out together, Dana was distraught by the question of why this thing had happened.

Randy — kind, sweet Randy. Why had Randy deceived her? How could he? He liked her, Dana. He showed it in a million ways. He even once told her he loved her. She hadn't wanted to hear that, she remembered, but he had said it. How could he have turned to Shelley?

The longer and faster she ran, the more Dana realized that her first shock and anger had turned into questions, one question after another, questions that pounded at her, questions she couldn't answer.

Evening shadows fell. The whole campus was going dark as Dana ran — hurt, confused, disturbed by something she tried to understand but couldn't even identify. Out of breath — from running? from the force of those whirling questions? — she slowed down, went from running to jogging and then to walking. She didn't consciously choose a direction to walk, except that she didn't want to go back to the dorm yet. She walked without hesitation but it was almost a surprise to her that when she stopped, she was standing at the door of the third house down on East Faculty Row, a small, white-trimmed, brick house with a beat-up red bicycle out front. Her hand was doing its thing before she even knew she had willed it to. It was lifting the thick, lion-head brass knocker.

Michael Frank came to the door wearing gray slacks, a blue shirt, one hand struggling with a blue polka-dot bow tie. A tie!

"Oh, Michael, you're dressed up. You're going somewhere. It's the weekend. You can't see me. I should have waited and gone to your office."

The blurted phrases were so unlike Dana that the school psychologist opened the door wide.

"Hey, Dana," he said warmly. "If you don't mind watching a grown man cry over a tie, come on in."

Dana took a deep breath, somewhat shakily, and entered the house.

"I've never seen you so dressed up, Michael," she said nervously.

His usual Canby attire was jeans, turtleneck, old lumber jacket and, in the cold, an old ski cap with dangling pompoms and "Berkeley," for Berkeley, his alma mater, written across it. She realized she had barged in on him at an inconvenient time; he obviously had a date. Dana wondered momentarily if it was with Alison. But she didn't care that she had barged in. She had been compelled to come to him.

"I'm off to Boston this evening," Michael said, "but I've got some time."

He led her into the parlor. Smiling, he gestured her to the old-fashioned horsehair sofa with the funny, carved mahogany legs and watched her settle herself. Then he pulled up its matching chair and gave her his full, most supportive attention. He waited for her to speak.

Dana looked trustingly at him. Earlier this winter she had had the world's biggest crush on Michael Frank. It had embarrassed her and exhilarated her and left her, finally, with new perceptions and an older friend she could rely on. Michael's dark, perceptive eyes, intent upon her now, the laugh lines crinkling his face, his low, rumbling voice all gave her deep, solid assurance.

"I just learned something. . . . I feel so humiliated." She stumbled on the words, looked down at her hands, then looked up. With someone else, she might have been flippant, made a joke to hide her misery, but Dana knew she didn't have to be on guard with Michael.

"I . . . I don't think I can handle it," she said.

"Go on," he said. His deep voice, his rugged face, were so unruffled, so calm, that the tight, hard knot of shock inside her finally started to loosen.

"My roommate Shelley's been going out with my boyfriend Randy," she said.

He sat upright, genuinely startled. "Well, that *is* a shocker," he said. "Tell me."

"I . . . I saw them . . . and Shelley admitted it . . . and Faith knew."

"How'd it happen, Dana?" Michael asked, his deep eyes probing hers.

"I don't know how," Dana answered. "That's what's been driving me crazy. That's what confuses me. I've just run miles trying to understand exactly that." She caught her breath. "And to think I sent her out with him the first time."

"You did what?" Dana was too busy with her own tumble of feelings to notice Michael's surprise.

"Asked her to go out with him."

Michael leaned forward, elbows on his knees, hands clasped. "Why'd you do that?" he asked.

"Why shouldn't I? I trusted her," Dana said indignantly.

"Start at the beginning, Dana, okay?" he said.

"There was nothing to it, Michael. It was a Friday night. I had a date to go to the movies with Randy. But I had a book report to do so I asked Shelley to go instead, to keep him company," Dana said.

"I see. Did Shelley want to go?" Michael asked.

"That's another part of what I don't understand," Dana said earnestly. "She didn't want to at all. She just did it as a favor to me. And then look what happened."

"You pressed her to go?" Michael persisted.

"Well, I couldn't, and Randy was already downstairs. . . ."

"Dana, why did you ask Shelley to go with him?"

"I told you. Because I had a book report," Dana answered.

"Think about that. If she didn't want to go, why did you urge her?"

"Because I couldn't. . . ." She stopped herself. She felt a little uncertain. Then a surprising idea came to her. "Because I didn't want to?" she asked Michael.

"What do you think?"

Dana thought hard for a moment, tried to remember exactly how she had felt that evening. "Maybe I didn't want to, maybe the book report was only an excuse," she said after a while, slowly, hesitantly. Then a wave of anger swept her.

"But they've been going out ever since, behind my back," she insisted.

Michael's voice was still calm. "Do you think that's what you might have wanted them to do?" he asked.

"No!" Dana cried, but she looked at him with a puzzled expression.

"That's something for you to think about, Dana," Michael said.

"Oh, Michael, I hate the way I feel. I thought I was so sensible and mature about everything . . . about Randy, for instance, but this. . . ."

"This . . . is going to make you do some hard thinking, huh?" He stood up, and she did, and they walked together to the front door. "If you want to talk some more about it, Dana, call Jane early Monday morning." Jane was his secretary. "She'll set up an appointment in my office for right away. Okay?" Dana nodded. "I've got terrific faith in you, Dana," he said, sending strength to her with his dark eyes.

* * *

After Dana ran out of Room 407, Faith stood listening to Shelley's sobbing for a few minutes, not knowing if she should approach her or not. Finally she walked over to Shelley and sat down on the edge of her mattress. She touched Shelley's shoulder gently.

"Don't you think it's time you talked about it, Shel?" she asked quietly.

"What's there to talk about? Dana thinks I'm a creep and I guess she's right."

"Well, I know you, Shelley, and you usually have reasons for doing the things you do. I think it would help *me*, if you tried to tell me why it happened."

"There isn't any reason," Shelley said, but Faith could tell by her expression that Shelley wasn't being completely honest.

"Are you in love with Randy?"

"No, it's not that," she answered slowly.

"Are you angry with Dana, jealous of her, something like that?"

"No!" Shelley almost yelled. "I mean, no, I was never angry with Dana. She begged me to go out with Randy that first time. I didn't want to, not because I knew something like this would happen, but just because it seemed kind of, well, you know, weird. But Randy and I had a great time on that first date. We found out we had so much in common and we really liked each other. Then I ran into him accidentally one day and we had fun again. That's when we realized we were attracted to each other. We went horseback riding once, just like Paul and I used to. . . ." Her voice trailed off.

"Dana should have known better," said Faith thoughtfully.

"Yeah," said Shelley. "Known better than to trust me." She looked as if she was going to start crying again.

"That's not what I meant, Shelley," Faith said. "I mean she should have known how much you and Randy have in common. She may have wanted this to happen and never even realized it herself."

"Do you mean it's just as much Dana's fault as mine?" Shelley asked, her eyes wide.

"It doesn't make too much sense otherwise, does it? I mean, I would never send Johnny out with anyone else. Would you want Tom or Paul to go out with another girl?"

"No, I don't think I would," Shelley answered. Both girls looked at each other. They looked puzzled and worried, but Shelley's eyes were no longer full of tears.

Long after she left Michael, Dana was asking herself the questions he suggested — Why did I ask Shelley to go out with Randy? Why didn't I want to go with him? What did I want to happen? — and coming up with surprising answers. How did she really feel about Randy? That was the first, most important thing to know.

I like him, she told herself as she walked

almost automatically up East Faculty Row
toward the birch grove. *I really think he's
great, but he's so different from me, I never
feel comfortable with him.* She thought about
what that meant. She began to compare the
feelings she had about Randy to those she had
had for Bret Harper, the Oakley Prep glamor
boy she had gone with earlier in the year. Bret
was certainly far from perfect. He'd played
the whole field of girls. She wouldn't even
want to go out with him again. But Bret
wasn't different the way Randy was. She tried
to imagine herself asking Shelley to take her
place on a date with Bret and knew she never
would do it. Why was that? she wondered.
Maybe it was because her feelings for Bret
had been so intense that she could never have
been able to share him with anyone else,
even for a moment. Randy, on the other hand,
never evoked such strong feelings of love —
or hate. Even now. Whatever it was she felt
for Randy, though — affection, caring, attraction — were real feelings. That she was sure
of. Somehow that knowledge cleared her head
a little.

Dana walked through the birch grove,
passed Charles House, the first in the row of
Canby Hall's three dormitories, and on to
Baker House. Soon she was standing in front
of her dorm, looking at the lights of the
lounge downstairs showing muted and warm
through the chintz curtains. She looked up to

the second and third stories. The light in the upstairs windows was sharper with the bright glow of overhead lights, of lamps on desks. Dana looked particularly at the two second-floor windows immediately above and a little to the right of the doorway. The lights were on in room 407. Dana paused before going in.

Dana never thought that mottos, slogans, or symbols could give real help when you needed it, but she found herself thinking "lioness" as she entered the dorm. The thought seemed actually to straighten her back and shoulders and hold her head high as she walked firmly down the hall to her room and went in to face Shelley Hyde, her roommate who had deceived her.

Dana felt it had been a lifetime since she stormed out of the room, shocked, to jog and cry, finally to see Michael, but it was as though time had frozen. Shelley was lying on her bed, almost exactly as she had been when Dana left, obviously still badly upset, her cheeks flushed from crying, her eyes puffy. Faith, in pajamas now, was slouched on the floor against her bed, almost in the same place she, too, had been when Dana left.

At first the three girls in the room were frozen in position, then Shelley jumped up and stood in front of Dana.

"Please forgive me, Dana," she said.

Dana looked at the earnest, blotched face

of her roommate. *How do I feel about Shelley?* she asked herself. That was the key question, the one as yet unanswered.

"I don't know, Shel," she said, and walked toward her bed, pulled off her jacket, tossed it toward the closet, sat down, and kicked off her running shoes. She sat limp at the edge of the bed. Faith, across the room, watched and listened.

"I will if I can," Dana said. "I'm not ready to talk about it right now."

Shelley turned and faced her. "I think you should forgive me," she said.

"Why?" Dana asked. She really wanted to know.

"Well, it was . . . in a funny way, the whole thing was your idea, Dana. Don't you remember I didn't want to go on your date with Randy? Remember how you insisted?"

"I remember asking you to go to a movie with my boyfriend, Shelley," Dana said angrily. "I don't remember asking you to sneak around behind my back with him and make a fool of me in front of the whole school. That's what I'd expect from Pamela, not someone who's supposed to be my friend."

"Dana, please. . . ." Shelley began.

"I said I don't want to talk about it now," Dana said, grabbing a small purse from her desk. She quickly ran out the door and down the stairs to the pay phone in the lobby. Her hands shaking, she put a coin in the slot, dialed, and waited for the ringing to begin and the phone to be answered.

"Randy? It's Dana."

"I was hoping you would call," said Randy quietly.

"Can I talk to you?" she asked.

"Sure," he answered. "On the phone?"

"No, in person."

"Okay. Want me to pick you up?"

"No, why don't we meet at Pizza Pete's? I'm leaving now."

"Great," said Randy. "I'll be there in —" He stopped, realizing that Dana had already hung up.

Randy stood up when he saw Dana enter the restaurant. He reached his arms out to give her a hug but she didn't respond. He touched her elbow lightly as he led her to the booth.

"The pizza should be ready in just a few minutes," he said brightly as they sat down. "I ordered a pepperoni with mushrooms and extra cheese."

"Sounds great," said Dana feebly.

"I don't know what else to say besides I'm sorry," Randy said after a pause. "It wasn't anything I had planned. You must know that, Dana. I never even really noticed Shelley before that night when you asked me to go out with —"

"Everyone's trying to tell me this is all my fault," Dana interrupted angrily. "If you and Shelley are so innocent, why did you have to sneak around?" she demanded. "If there was nothing wrong with what you were doing, why didn't you just tell me about it?"

"I never said there wasn't anything wrong with it. It *was* wrong and it never should have happened. I care about you, Dana, and you're the one I want to keep seeing, not Shelley. I hope you'll be able to forgive me."

Suddenly, everything started to make sense. Randy was right. It never should have happened and it never would have, if she, Dana, had not wanted it to. Now she knew what Michael, Shelley, Randy, and much earlier Faith — dear, smart Faith — had been trying to tell her. She knew absolutely that she had wanted Shelley and Randy to go together, had felt that they would be much better together than she and Randy were. Randy wanted to spend the rest of his life on his family's ranch, something that she could never begin to comprehend, but that Shelley understood instinctively.

Shelley had been formed by the small towns and farms, by 4-H clubs and church socials, the stability and homogeneity of the Midwest. Dana had been shaped by the exact opposite, by New York, the restless, biggest city, where you heard every language in the world on the street, where funk and elegance went together, and rush and change were the rule. The core of her felt the great difference between herself and Shelley, and herself and Randy.

She reached her arms across the table and cupped Randy's face in her hands. "I *do* forgive you. Will you forgive me, too?"

"What for, Dana?" he asked.

"For wanting you to go out with Shelley in the first place."

"Oh, it wasn't *that* big a sacrifice," said Randy, teasing her.

Dana looked at him sharply for a moment and then started laughing. Everything was going to be okay. Randy caught her eye and they both broke up even harder. Dana didn't know if she was going to be able to stop laughing long enough to eat the pizza that was just being brought to the table. Suddenly she had an idea.

"Randy, would you mind awfully if I brought this pizza home for my roommates? I haven't had a talk with Shelley and Faith yet, and I feel like doing it right now. Pizza might make the conversation flow a little more smoothly," she said with a grin.

"As a matter of fact, I had just finished one of my mother's huge snacks when you called," he said. "You know me, I can always eat, but even I am feeling a little full right now."

"Good," said Dana, standing up. "Let's go then."

"But I will see you some time soon, I hope," said Randy, looking at her expectantly.

"Of course, you will," she said, linking arms with him as they walked through the door and towards Randy's truck.

Dana stood in the doorway of Room 407, looking curiously formal. She approached Shelley and the two girls faced each other. "I didn't really remember how this whole thing started, Shel, but I do now," she said slowly, squarely. "I forgive you."

The girls looked somberly into each other's eyes. Then they both smiled.

"Thanks," Shelley said, sighing with relief. "It was just awful. I think Randy was just a kind of substitute for Paul back home. He reminded me of all the things I missed but didn't even really know I missed."

"Never mind," Dana said. "It was me. I set it up with my own dumb feelings and actions."

"Not dumb, Dana," Faith protested.

"Will you take very extremely mixed-up?"

"Yep," said Faith, and at last the atmosphere in the room cleared. Dana and Shelley hugged each other.

"Wow," said Shelley, collapsing on the floor. "Never again. Never, never, *never* again." Then she sat up. "I just decided something else," she said. "All men do is get a girl in trouble. I think I'm going to be a nun."

"You're not even Catholic," Dana said.

"I could convert," Shelley answered. They all laughed, but then Dana went quickly serious.

"Shel, this isn't really the first time and I don't think it's going to be the last time we have problems between us," she said.

"I guess I agree, Dana," Shelley said, "but that doesn't mean I don't love you. I do."

"I love you, too, Shel. It's just that our friendship seems to have some terrific built-in conflicts."

"Comes with the territory, children," Faith said. "Big-city girl, small-city girl, school-mates, roommates."

"I'll buy that," Dana said.

"Me, too," Shelley said.

"Now, anybody interested in food?" Dana asked, pointing to the pizza box that lay on the floor by the doorway.

Faith's and Shelley's eyes lit up. They had been so nervous when Dana walked into the room that they hadn't even noticed the white box she had been carrying. Suddenly all three girls were famished. Dana brought the pizza to the center of the room and they all dug into it happily. Faith brought three cans of diet soda from the stack on the window sill and gave each girl one. Pop, pop, pop — three cans opened and Faith proposed a toast.

"To friendship," she said, and the three girls looked at each other, smiled, and drank deeply.